William Jones

Poems, Consisting Chiefly of Translations from the Asiatick Languages.

To which are Added two Essays. Second Edition

William Jones

Poems, Consisting Chiefly of Translations from the Asiatick Languages.
To which are Added two Essays. Second Edition

ISBN/EAN: 9783744764834

Printed in Europe, USA, Canada, Australia, Japan

Cover: Foto ©Andreas Hilbeck / pixelio.de

More available books at **www.hansebooks.com**

P O E M S,

CONSISTING CHIEFLY

OF

TRANSLATIONS

FROM THE

ASIATICK LANGUAGES.

TO WHICH ARE ADDED

TWO ESSAYS;

I. On the Poetry of the Eastern Nations.
II. On the Arts, commonly called Imitative.

———— *Juvat integros accedere fontes,*
Atque haurire, juvatque novos decerpere flores. LUCR.

By SIR WILLIAM JONES.

THE SECOND EDITION.

LONDON:

Printed by W. BOWYER and J. NICHOLS;

For N. CONANT (Successor to MR. WHISTON),
in FLEET STREET.

M DCC LXXVII.

TO

THE RIGHT HONOURABLE

THE COUNTESS SPENCER,

THESE EASTERN PIECES,

AND, PARTICULARLY,

THE POEM OF

SOLIMA,

ARE MOST RESPECTFULLY

INSCRIBED

BY HER LADYSHIP'S

MOST OBLIGED

AND FAITHFUL SERVANT,

THE AUTHOR.

THE CONTENTS.

A 3 THE

THE

PREFACE.

THE reader will probably expect, that, before I present him with the following miscellany, I should give some account of the pieces contained in it; and should prove the authenticity of those *Eastern* originals, from which I profess to have translated them: indeed, so many productions, invented in *France*, have been offered to the publick as genuine translations from the languages of *Asia*, that I should have wished,

a 4   for

for my own fake, to clear my publication from
the flighteft fufpicion of impofture; but there is a
circumftance peculiarly hard in the prefent cafe;
namely, that, were I to produce the *originals* themfelves, it would be impoffible to perfuade fome
men, that even *they* were not forged for the purpofe, like the pretended language of *Formofa.* I
fhall, however, attempt in this fhort preface to
fatisfy the reader's expectations.

The firft poem in the collection, called. *Solima,* is,
not a regular tranflation from the *Arabick* language;
but moft of the figures, fentiments, and defcriptions in it, were really taken from the poets of
Arabia: for when I was reading fome of their
verfes on benevolence and hofpitality, which they
juftly confider as their moft amiable virtues, I
felected thofe paffages, that feemed moft likely
to run into our meafure, and connected them in
fuch a manner as to form one continued piece,
which I fuppofe to be written in praife of an *Arabian* princefs, who had built a *caravanfera* with
pleafant

pleafant gardens for the refreſhment of travellers
and pilgrims; an act of munificence not un-
common in *Aſia*. I ſhall trouble the reader with
only one of the original paſſages, from which he
may form a tolerable judgement of the reſt:

Kad alama e'ddhaiſo wa'l mojteduno
Idha aghbara ofkon wahabbat ſhemalan,
Wakbalat an auladiha elmordbiato,
Wa lam tar ainon lemoznin belalan,
Beenca conto 'errabio el moghitho
Leman yâtarica, waconto themalan,
Waconto' nehara behi ſhemſoho,
Waconto dagiyyi' lleili fihi helalan.

that is; * *the ſtranger and the pilgrim well know,*
when the ſky is dark, and the north-wind rages,
when the mothers leave their ſucking infants, when
no moiſture can be ſeen in the clouds, that thou art
bountiful to them as the ſpring, that thou art their
chief ſupport, that thou art a ſun to them by day, and
a moon in the cloudy night.

* See this paſſage verſified, *Solima*, line 71. &c.

The

The hint of the next poem, or *The Palace of Fortune*, was taken from an *Indian* tale, tranflated a few years ago from the *Perfian* by a very ingenious gentleman in the fervice of the *India-company*; but I have added feveral defcriptions, and epifodes from other *Eaftern* writers, have given a different moral to the whole piece, and have made fome other alterations in it, which may be feen by any one, who will take the pains to compare it with the ftory of *Rofhana*, in the fecond volume of the tales of *Inatulla*.

I have taken a ftill greater liberty with the moral allegory, which, in imitation of the *Perfian* poet *Nezámi*, I have entitled *The Seven Fountains*; the general fubject of it was borrowed from a ftory in a collection of tales by *Ebn Arabfhah*, a native of *Damafcus*, who flourifhed in the fifteenth century, and wrote feveral other works in a very polifhed ftyle, the moft celebrated of which is *An hiftory of the life of Tamerlane* : but I have
                                        ingrafted

ingrafted upon the principal allegory an epifode from the *Arabian* tales of * *a thoufand and one nights*, a copy of which work in *Arabick* was procured for me by a learned friend at *Aleppo*.

The fong, which follows, was firft printed at the end of a *Perfian* grammar; but, for the fatif-faction of thofe who may have any doubt of its being genuine, it feemed proper to fet down the original of it in *Roman* characters at the bottom of the page. The ode of *Petrarch* was added, that the reader might compare the manner of the *Afiatick* poets with that of the *Italians*, many of whom have written in the true fpirit of the *Eafterns:* fome of the *Perfian* fongs have a ftrik-ing refemblance to the fonnets of *Petrarch*; and even the form of thofe little amatory poems was, I believe, brought into *Europe* by the *Arabians:* one would almoft imagine the following lines to be tranflated from the *Perfian*,

* See the ftory of Prince *Agib*, or the *third Calandar* in the *Arabian tales*, Night 57. &c.

Aura,

Aura, che quelle chiome bionde e crespe
Circondi, e movi, e se' mossa da lorò
Soavemente, è spargi quel dolce oro,
E poi 'l raccogli, e'n bei nodi l'increspe.

since there is scarce a page in the works of *Hafez*
and *Jami*, in which the same image, of *the breeze*
playing with the tresses of a beautiful girl, is not
agreeably and variously expressed.

The elegy on the death of *Laura* was inserted
with the same view of forming a comparison
between the *Oriental* and the *Italian* poetry:
the description of the fountain of *Valchiusa*,
or *Vallis Clausa*, which was close to *Petrarch's*
house, was added to the elegy in the year
1769, and was composed on the very spot,
which I could not forbear visiting, when I passed
by *Avignon*.

The *Turkish* Ode on the Spring was selected
from many others in the same language, writ-

ten

ten by *Mefihi,* a poet of great repute at *Conftanti-nople,* who lived in the reign of *Soliman the Second,* or *the Lawgiver:* it is not unlike the *Vigil of Venus,* which has been afcribed to *Catullus;* the meafure of it is nearly the fame with that of the *Latin* poem; and it has, like that, a lively burden at the end of every ftanza: the works of *Mefihi* are preferved in the archives of the *Royal Society.*

It will be needlefs, I hope, to apologize for the *Paftoral,* and the poem upon *Chefs,* which were done as early as at the age of fixteen or feventeen years, and were faved from the fire, in preference to a great many others, becaufe they feemed more correctly verfified than the reft.

It muft not be fuppofed, from my zeal for the literature of *Afia,* that I mean to place it in competition with the beautiful productions of the *Greeks* and *Romans;* for I am convinced, that, whatever changes we make in our opinions, we always re-

turn

urn to the writings of the ancients, as to the ſtandard of true taſte.

If the novelty of the following poems ſhould recommend them to the favour of the reader, it may, probably, be agreeable to him to know, that there are many others of equal or ſuperior merit, which have never appeared in any language of *Europe*; and I am perſuaded that a writer, acquainted with the originals, might imitate them very happily in his native tongue, and that the publick would not be diſpleaſed to ſee the genuine compoſitions of *Arabia* and *Perſia* in an *Engliſh* dreſs. The heroick poem of *Ferduſi* might be verſified as eaſily as the *Iliad*, and I ſee no reaſon why *the delivery of Perſia by Cyrus* ſhould not be a ſubjeſt as intereſting to us, as *the anger of Achilles*, or *the wandering of Ulyſſes*. The Odes of *Hafez*, and of *Meſihi*, would ſuit our lyrick meaſures as well as thoſe aſcribed to *Anacreon*; and the ſeven *Arabick* elegies, that were hung up in the temple of *Mecca*, and of which there are ſeve-
ral

ral fine copies at *Oxford,* would, no doubt, be highly acceptable to the lovers of antiquity, and the admirers of native genius: but when I propofe a tranflation of thefe *Oriental* pieces, as a work likely to meet with fuccefs, I only mean to invite my readers, who have leifure and induftry, to the ftudy of the languages, in which they are written, and am very far from infinuating that I have the remoteft defign of performing any part of the tafk myfelf; for, to fay the truth, I fhould not have fuffered even the following trifles to fee the light, if I were not very defirous of recommending to the learned world a fpecies of literature, which abounds with fo many new expreffions, new images, and new inventions.

SOLI-

S O L I M A,

AN ARABIAN ECLOGUE,

Written in the Year 1768.

YE maids of Aden, hear a loftier tale
    Than e'er was fung in meadow, bower, or dale.
The fmiles of Abelah, and Maia's eyes,
Where beauty plays, and love in flumber lies;
The fragrant hyacinths of Azza's hair,
That wanton with the laughing fummer-air;
Love-tinctur'd cheeks, whence rofes feek their bloom,
And lips, from which the Zephyr fteals perfume;
Invite no more the wild, unpolifh'd lay,
But fly like dreams before the morning ray.

B

Then

Then farewel, love! and farewel, youthful fires!
A nobler warmth my kindled breaft infpires.
Far bolder notes the liftening wood fhall fill:
Flow fmooth, ye rivulets; and, ye gales, be ftill.

See yon fair groves that o'er Amana rife,
And with their fpicy breath embalm the fkies;
Where every breeze fheds incenfe o'er the vales,
And every fhrub the fcent of mufk exhales!
See through yon opening glade a glittering fcene,
Lawns ever gay, and meadows ever green!
Then afk the groves, and afk the vocal bowers,
Who deck'd their fpiry tops with blooming flowers,
Taught the blue ftream o'er fandy vales to flow,
And the brown wild with livelieft hues to glow?
*Fair Solima! the hills and dales will fing;
Fair Solima! the diftant echoes ring.
But not with idle fhows of vain delight,
To charm the foul, or to beguile the fight;
At noon on banks of pleafure to repofe,
Where bloom intwin'd the lily, pink, and rofe;

---

* It was not eafy in this part of the tranflation to avoid a turn
fimilar to that of Pope in the known defcription of the Man of
Rofs.

Not

Not in proud piles to heap the nightly feaft,
Till morn with pearls has deck'd the glowing caft;—
Ah! not for this fhe taught thofe bowers to rife,
And bade all Eden fpring before our eyes:
Far other thoughts her heavenly mind employ,
(Hence, empty pride! and hence, delufive joy!)
To cheer with fweet repaft the fainting gueft;
To lull the weary on the couch of reft;
To warm the traveller numb'd with winter's cold;
The young to cherifh, to fupport the old;
The fad to comfort, and the weak protect;
The poor to fhelter, and the loft direct:—
Thefe are her cares, and this her glorious tafk;
Can heaven a nobler give, or mortals afk?

Come to thefe groves, and thefe life-breathing glades,
Ye friendlefs orphans, and ye dowerlefs maids!
With eager hafte your mournful manfions leave,
Ye weak, that tremble; and, ye fick, that grieve;
Here fhall foft tents, o'er flowery lawns difplay'd,
At night defend you, and at noon o'erfhade;
Here rofy health the fweets of life will fhower,
And new delights beguile each varied hour.

Mourns there a widow, bath'd in ftreaming tears?
Stoops there a fire beneath the weight of years?
Weeps there a maid, in pining fadnefs left,
Of tender parents, and of hope, bereft?
To Solima their forrows they bewail;
To Solima they pour their plaintive tale.
She hears; and, radiant as the ftar of day,
Through the thick foreft gains her eafy way:
She afks what cares the joylefs train opprefs,
What ficknefs waftes them, or what wants diftrefs;
And, as they mourn, fhe fteals a tender figh,
Whilft all her foul fits melting in her eye:
Then with a finile the healing balm beftows,
And fheds a tear of pity o'er their woes,
Which, as it drops, fome foft-eyed angel bears
Transform'd to pearl, and in his bofom wears.

When, chill'd with fear, the trembling pilgrim roves
Through pathlefs deferts, and through tangled groves,
Where mantling darknefs fpreads her dragon wing,
And birds of death their fatal dirges fing,
While vapours pale a dreadful glimmering caft,
And thrilling horrour howls in every blaft;

She

She cheers his gloom with ftreams of burfting light,
By day a fun, a beaming moon by night;
Darts through the quivering fhades her heavenly ray,
And fpreads with rifing flowers his folitary way.

Ye heavens, for this in fhowers of fweetnefs fhed
Your mildeft influence o'er her favour'd head!
Long may her name, which diftant climes fhall praife,
Live in our notes, and bloffom in our lays!
And, like an odorous plant, whofe blufhing flower
Paints every dale, and fweetens every bower,
Borne to the fkies in clouds of foft perfume
For ever flourifh, and for ever bloom!
Thefe grateful fongs, ye maids and youths, renew,
While frefh-blown violets drink the pearly dew;
O'er Azib's banks while love-lorn damfels rove,
And gales of fragrance breathe from Hager's grove.

So fung the youth, whofe fweetly-warbled ftrains
Fair Mena heard, and Saba's fpicy plains.
Sooth'd with his lay, the ravifh'd air was calm,
The winds fcarce whifper'd o'er the waving palm;
The camels bounded o'er the flowery lawn,
Like the fwift oftrich, or the fportful fawn;

Their

Their filken bands the liftening rofe-buds rent,
And twin'd their bloffoms round his vocal tent:
He fung, till on the bank the moonlight flept,
And clofing flowers beneath the night-dew wept;
Then ceas'd, and flumber'd in the lap of reft
Till the fhrill lark had left his low-built neft.
Now haftes the fwain to tune his rapturous tales
In other meadows, and in other vales.

T H E

THE

PALACE OF FORTUNE,

AN INDIAN TALE.

Written in the Year 1769.

M ILD was the vernal gale, and calm the day,
When Maia near a cryſtal fountain lay,
Young Maia, faireſt of the blue-eyed maids,
That rov'd at noon in Tibet's muſky ſhades;
But, haply, wandering through the fields of air,
Some fiend had whiſper'd—Maia, thou art fair!
Hence ſwelling pride had fill'd her ſimple breaſt,
And riſing paſſions robb'd her mind of reſt;

In

In courts and glittering towers ſhe wiſh'd to dwell,
And ſcorn'd her labouring parent's lowly cell,
And now, as gazing o'er the glaſſy ſtream,
She ſaw her blooming cheek's reflected beam,
Her treſſes brighter than the morning ſky,
And the mild radiance of her ſparkling eye,
Low ſighs and trickling tears by turns ſhe ſtole,
And thus diſcharg'd the anguiſh of her ſoul:
" Why glow thoſe cheeks, if unadmir'd they glow?
" Why flow thoſe treſſes, if unprais'd they flow ?
" Why dart thoſe eyes their liquid ray ſerene,
" Unfelt their influence, and their light unſeen ?
" Ye heavens ! was that love-breathing boſom made
" To warm dull groves, and cheer the lonely glade ?
" Ah, no: thoſe bluſhes, that enchanting face,
" Some tap'ſtried hall, or gilded bower, might grace ;
" Might deck the ſcenes, where love and pleaſure reign,
" And fire with amorous flames the youthful train."

    While thus ſhe ſpoke, a ſudden blaze of light
Shot through the clouds, and ſtruck her dazzled ſight,
She rais'd her head, aſtoniſh'd, to the ſkies,
And veil'd with trembling hands her aching eyes ;

                                        When

When through the yielding air fhe faw from far
A goddefs gliding in a golden car,
That foon defcended on the flowery lawn,
By two fair yokes of ftarry peacocks drawn :
A thoufand nymphs with many a fprightly glance
Form'd round the radiant wheels an airy dance,
Celeftial fhapes ! in fluid light array'd;
Like twinkling ftars their beamy fandals play'd;
Their lucid mantles glitter'd in the fun,
(Webs half fo bright the filkworm never fpun)
Tranfparent robes, that bore the rainbow's hue,
And finer than the nets of pearly dew
That morning fpreads o'er every opening flower,
When fportive fummer decks his bridal bower.

The queen herfelf, too fair for mortal fight,
Sat in the centre of encircling light.
Soon with foft touch fhe rais'd the trembling maid,
And by her fide in filent flumber laid :
Straight the gay birds difplay'd their fpangled train,
And flew refulgent through th' aerial plain ;
The fairy band their fhining pinions fpread,
And, as they rofe, frefh gales of fweetnefs fhed ;

Fann'd

Fann'd with their flowing fkirts, the fky was mild;
And heaven's blue fields with brighter radiance fmil'd.

Now in a garden deck'd with verdant bowers
The glittering car defcends on bending flowers:
The goddefs ftill with looks divinely fair
Surveys the fleeping object of her care;
Then o'er her cheek her magick finger lays,
Soft as the gale that o'er a violet plays,
And thus in founds, that favour'd mortals hear,.
She gently whifpers in her ravifh'd ear:

" Awake, fweet maid, and view this charming fcene
" For ever beauteous, and for ever green;
" Here living rills of pureft nectar flow
" O'er meads that with unfading flowerets glow;
" Here amorous gales their fcented wings difplay,
" Mov'd by the breath of ever-blooming May;
" Here in the lap of pleafure fhalt thou reft,
" Our lov'd companion, and our honour'd gueft."

The damfel hears the heavenly notes diftil,
Like melting fnow, or like a vernal rill.

She

She lifts her head, and, on her arm reclin'd,
Drinks the fweet accents in her grateful mind :
On all around fhe turns her roving eyes,
And views the fplendid fcene with glad furprize;
Frefh lawns, and funny banks, and rofeate bowers,
Hills white with flocks, and meadows gemm'd with flowers;
Cool fhades, a fure defence from fummer's ray,
And filver brooks, where wanton damfels play,
Which with foft notes their dimpled cryftal roll'd
O'er colour'd fhells and fands of native gold ;
A rifing fountain play'd from every ftream,
Smil'd as it rofe, and caft a tranfient gleam,
Then, gently falling in a vocal fhower,
Bath'd every fhrub, and fprinkled every flower,
That on the banks, like many a lovely bride,
View'd in the liquid glafs their blufhing pride;
Whilft on each branch, with purple bloffoms hung,
The fportful birds their joyous defcant fung.

While Maia, thus entranc'd in fweet delight,
With each gay object fed her eager fight,
The goddefs mildly caught her willing hand,
And led her trembling o'er the flowery land.

Soon

Soon fhe beheld, where through an opening glade
A fpacious lake its clear expanfe difplay'd;
In mazy curls the flowing jafper wav'd
O'er its fmooth bed with polifh'd agate pav'd;
And on a rock of ice, by magick rais'd,
High in the midft a gorgeous palace blaz'd;
The funbeams on the gilded portals glanc'd,
Play'd on the fpires, and on the turrets danc'd;
To four bright gates four ivory bridges led,
With pearls illumin'd, and with rofes fpread:
And now, more radiant than the morning fun,
Her eafy way the gliding goddefs won;
Still by her hand fhe held the fearful maid,
And, as fhe pafs'd, the fairies homage paid:
They enter'd ftraight the fumptuous palace-hall,
Where filken tapeftry emblaz'd the wall,
Refulgent tiffue, of an heavenly woof;
And gems unnumber'd fparkled on the roof,
On whofe blue arch the flaming diamonds play'd,
As on a fky with living ftars inlay'd;
Of precious diadems a regal ftore,
With globes and fceptres, ftrew'd the porphyry floor;
Rich vefts of eaftern kings around were fpread,
And glittering zones a ftarry luftre fhed:

But

But Maia moſt admir'd the pearly ſtrings,
Gay bracelets, golden chains, and ſparkling rings.

High in the centre of the palace ſhone,
Suſpended in mid-air, an opal throne:
To this the queen aſcends with royal pride,
And ſets the favour'd damſel by her ſide.
Around the throne in myſtick order ſtand
The fairy train, and wait her high command;
When thus ſhe ſpeaks: (the maid attentive ſips
Each word that flows, like nectar, from her lips.)

  " Favourite of heaven, my much-lov'd Maia, know,
" From me all joys, all earthly bleſſings, flow:
" Me ſuppliant men imperial Fortune call,
" The mighty empreſs of yon rolling ball:
(She rais'd her finger, and the wondering maid
At diſtance hung the duſky globe ſurvey'd,
Saw the round earth with foaming oceans vein'd,
And labouring clouds on mountain tops ſuſtain'd.)
" To me has fate the pleaſing taſk aſſign'd
" To rule the various thoughts of humankind;
 . " To catch each riſing wiſh, each ardent prayer,
" And ſome to grant, and ſome to waſte in air.

                                    " Know

" Know farther; as I rang'd the cryſtal ſky,

" I ſaw thee near the murmuring fountain lie;

" Mark'd the rough ſtorm that gather'd in thy breaſt,

" And knew what care thy joyleſs ſoul oppreſt.

" Straight I reſolv'd to bring thee quick relief,

" Eaſe every weight, and ſoften every grief;

" If in this court contented thou canſt live,

" And taſte the joys theſe happy gardens give:

" But fill thy mind with vain deſires no more,.

" And view without a wiſh yon ſhining ſtore:

" Soon ſhall a numerous train before me bend,

" And kneeling votaries my ſhrine attend;

" Warn'd by their empty vanities beware,

" And ſcorn the folly of each human prayer."

She ſaid; and ſtraight a damſel of her train

With tender fingers touch'd a golden chain.

Now a ſoft bell delighted Maia hears,

That ſweetly trembles on her liſtening ears;

Through the calm air the melting numbers float,

And wanton echo lengthens every note.

Soon through the dome a mingled hum aroſe,

Like the ſwift ſtream that o'er a valley flows;

Now louder ſtill it grew, and ſtill more loud,
As diſtant thunder breaks the burſting cloud:
Through the four portals ruſh'd a various throng,
That like a wintry torrent pour'd along:
A croud of every tongue, and every hue,
Toward the bright throne with eager rapture flew.
* A lovely ſtripling ſtepp'd before the reſt
With haſty pace, and tow'rd the goddeſs preſt;
His mien was graceful, and his looks were mild,
And in his eye celeſtial ſweetneſs ſmil'd:
Youth's purple glow, and beauty's roſy beam,
O'er his ſmooth cheeks diffus'd a lively gleam;
The floating ringlets of his muſky hair
Wav'd on the boſom of the wanton air:
With modeſt grace the goddeſs he addreſt,
And thoughtleſs thus preferr'd his fond requeſt.

" Queen of the world, whoſe wide-extended ſway,
" Gay youth, firm manhood, and cold age obey,
" Grant me, while life's freſh blooming roſes ſmile,
" The day with varied pleaſures to beguile;
" Let me on beds of dewy flowers recline,
" And quaff with glowing lips the ſparkling wine;

* Pleaſure.

" Grant

" Grant me to feed on beauty's rifled charms,

" And clasp a willing damsel in my arms ;

" Her bosom fairer than a hill of snow,

" And gently bounding like a playful roe;

" Her lips more fragrant than the summer air,

" And sweet as Scythian musk her hyacinthine hair;

" Let new delights each dancing hour employ,

" Sport follow sport, and joy succeed to joy."

The goddess grants the simple youth's request,

And mildly thus accosts her lovely guest:

" On that smooth mirror, full of magick light,

" Awhile, dear Maia, fix thy wandering sight."

She looks ; and in th' enchanted cryftal sees

A bower o'er-canopied with tufted trees:

The wanton stripling lies beneath the shade,

And by his side reclines a blooming maid;

O'er her fair limbs a silken mantle flows,

Through which her youthful beauty softly glows,

And part conceal'd, and part disclos'd to sight,

Through the thin texture casts a ruddy light,

As the ripe clusters of the mantling vine

Beneath the verdant foliage faintly shine,

And,

And, fearing to be view'd by envious day,
Their glowing tints unwillingly difplay.

The youth, while joy fits fparkling in his eyes,
Pants on her neck, and on her bofom dies;
From her fmooth cheek nectareous dew he fips,
And all his foul comes breathing to his lips.
But Maia turns her modeft eyes away,
And blufhes to behold their amorous play.

She looks again, and fees with fad furprize
On the clear glafs far different fcenes arife:
The bower, which late outfhone the rofy morn,
O'erhung with weeds fhe faw, and rough with thorn;
With ftings of afps the leaflefs plants were wreath'd,
And curling adders gales of venom breath'd:
Low fat the ftripling on the faded ground,
And in a mournful knot his arms were bound;
His eyes, that fhot before a funny beam,
Now fcarcely fhed a faddening, dying gleam;
Faint as a glimmering taper's wafted light,
Or a dull ray that ftreaks the cloudy night:
His cryftal vafe was on the pavement roll'd,
And from the bank was fall'n his cup of gold;

C   From

From which th' envenom'd dregs of deadly hue
Flow'd on the ground in ftreams of baleful dew,
And, flowly ftealing through the wither'd bower,
Poifon'd each plant, and blafted every flower:
Fled were his flaves, and fled his yielding fair,
And each gay phantom was diffolv'd in air;
Whilft in their place was left a ruthlefs train,
Defpair, and grief, remorfe, and raging pain.

Afide the damfel turns her weeping eyes,
And fad reflections in her bofom rife;
To whom thus mildly fpeaks the radiant queen:
" Take fage example from this moral fcene;
" See, how vain pleafures fting the lips they kifs,
" How afps are hid beneath the bowers of blifs!
" Whilft ever fair the flower of temperance blows,
" Unchang'd her leaf, and without thorn her rofe;
" Smiling fhe darts her glittering branch on high,
" And fpreads her fragrant bloffoms to the fky."

* Next tow'rd the throne fhe faw a knight advance;
Erect he ftood, and fhook a quivering lance;

* Glory.

A fiery

A fiery dragon on his helmet fhone;
And on his buckler beam'd a golden fun;
O'er his broad bofom blaz'd his jointed mail
With many a gem, and many a fhining fcale;
He trod the founding-floor with princely mien,
And thus with haughty words addrefs'd the queen:
" Let falling kings beneath my javelin bleed,
" And bind my temples with a victor's meed;
" Let every realm that feels the folar ray,
" Shrink at my frown, and own my regal fway:
" Let Ind's rich banks declare my deathlefs fame,
" And trembling Ganges dread my potent name."

The queen confented to the warriour's pray'r,
And his bright banners floated in the air:
He bade his darts in fteely tempefts fly;
Flames burft the clouds, and thunder fhake the fky;
Death aim'd his lance, earth trembled at his nod,
And crimfon conqueft glow'd where'er he trod.

And now the damfel, fix'd in deep amaze,
Th' enchanted glafs with eager look furveys:
She fees the hero in his dufky tent,
His guards retir'd; his glimmering taper fpent;

C 2

His

His fpear, vain inftrument of dying praife,
On the rich floor with idle ftate he lays;
His gory falchion near his pillow ftood,
And ftain'd the ground with drops of purple blood;
A bufy page his nodding helm unlac'd,
And on the couch his fcaly hauberk plac'd:
Now on the bed his weary limbs he throws,
Bath'd in the balmy dew of foft repofe:
In dreams he rufhes o'er the gloomy field,
He fees new armies fly, new heroes yield;
Warm with the vigorous conflict he appears,
And ev'n in flumber feems to move the fpheres.
But lo! the faithlefs page, with ftealing tread,
Advances to the champion's naked head;
With his fharp dagger wounds his bleeding breaft,
And fteeps his eyelids in eternal reft:
Then cries, (and waves the fteel that drops with gore)
" The tyrant dies; oppreffion is no more."

* Now came an aged fire with trembling pace;
Sunk were his eyes, and pale his ghaftly face;
A ragged weed of dufky hue he wore,
And on his back a ponderous coffer bore.

* Riches.

The

The queen with faltering fpeech he thus addreft :
" O, fill with gold thy true adorer's cheft!"

" Behold, faid fhe, and wav'd her powerful hand,
" Where yon rich hills in glittering order ftand :
" There load thy coffer with the golden ftore ;
" Then bear it full away, and afk no more."

With eager fteps he took his hafty way,
Where the bright coin in heaps unnumber'd lay ;
There hung enamour'd o'er the gleaming fpoil,
Scoop'd the gay drofs, and bent beneath the toil.
But bitter was his anguifh, to behold
The coffer widen, and its fides unfold :
And every time he heap'd the darling ore,
His greedy cheft grew larger than before ;
Till, fpent with pain, and falling o'er his hoard,
With his fharp fteel his maddening breaft he gor'd :
On the lov'd heap he caft his clofing eye,
Contented on a golden couch to die.

A ftripling, with the fair adventure pleas'd,
Stepp'd forward, and the maffy coffer feiz'd ;

But

But with furprize he faw the ftores decay,
And all the long-fought treafures melt away:
In winding ftreams the liquid metal roll'd,
And through the palace ran a flood of gold.

   * Next to the fhrine advanc'd a reverend fage,
Whofe beard was hoary with the froft of age ;
His few gray locks a fable fillet bound,
And his dark mantle flow'd along the ground :
Grave was his port, yet fhow'd a bold neglect,
And fill'd the young beholder with refpect ;
Time's envious hand had plough'd his wrinkled face,
Yet on thofe wrinkles fat fuperiour grace ;
Still full of fire appear'd his vivid eye,
Darted quick beams, and feem'd to pierce the fky.
At length, with gentle voice and look ferene,
He wav'd his hand, and thus addrefs'd the queen :

   " Twice forty winters tip my beard with fnow,
" And age's chilling gufts around me blow :
" In early youth, by contemplation led,
" With high purfuits my flatter'd thoughts were fed ;

         * Knowledge.

                            To

, " To nature firft my labours were confin'd,

" And all her charms were open'd to my mind,

" Each flower that gliften'd in the morning dew,

" And every fhrub that in the foreft grew :

" From earth to heaven I caft my wondering eyes,

" Saw funs unnumber'd fparkle in the skies,

" Mark'd the juft progrefs of each rolling fphere,

" Defcrib'd the feafons, and reform'd the year.

" At length fublimer ftudies I began,

" And fix'd my level'd telefcope on man ;

" Knew all his powers, and all his paffions trac'd,

" What virtue rais'd him, and what vice debas'd :

" But when I faw his knowledge fo confin'd,

" So vain his wifhes, and fo weak his mind,

" His foul, a bright obfcurity at beft,

" And rough with tempefts his afflicted breaft,

" His life, a flower ere evening fure to fade,

" His higheft joys, the fhadow of a fhade ;

" To thy fair court I took my weary way,

" Bewail my folly, and heaven's laws obey,

" Confefs my feeble mind for prayers unfit,

" And to my maker's will my foul fubmit :

" Great emprefs of yon orb that roll's below,

" On me the laft beft gift of heaven beftow."

He

He fpoke: a fudden cloud his fenfes ftole,
And thickening darknefs fwam o'er all his foul;
His vital fpark her earthly cell forfook,
And into air her fleeting progrefs took.

Now from the throng a deafening found was heard,
And all at once their various prayers preferr'd;
The goddefs, wearied with the noify croud,
Thrice wav'd her filver wand, and fpoke aloud:
" Our ears no more with vain petitions tire,
" But take unheard whate'er you firft defire."
She faid: each wifh'd, and what he wifh'd obtain'd;
And wild confufion in the palace reign'd.

But Maia, now grown fenfelefs with delight,
Caft on an emerald ring her roving fight;
And, ere fhe could furvey the reft with care,
Wifh'd on her hand the precious gem to wear,

Sudden the palace vanifh'd from her fight,
And the gay fabrick melted into night;
But, in its place, fhe view'd with weeping eyes
Huge rocks around her, and fharp cliffs arife;

She

She fat deferted on the naked fhore,
Saw the curl'd waves, and heard the tempeft roar;
Whilft on her finger fhone the fatal ring,
A weak defence from hunger's pointed fting,
From fad remorfe, from comfortlefs defpair,
And all the painful family of care!
Frantick with grief her rofy cheek fhe tore,
And rent her locks, her darling charge no more:
But when the night his raven wing had fpread,
And hung with fable every mountain's head,
Her tender limbs were numb'd with biting cold,
And round her feet the curling billows roll'd;
With trembling arms a rifted crag fhe grafp'd,
And the rough rock with hard embraces clafp'd.

While thus fhe ftood, and made a piercing moan,
By chance her emerald touch'd the rugged ftone;
That moment gleam'd from heaven a golden ray,
And taught the gloom to counterfeit the day:
A winged youth, for mortal eyes too fair,
Shot like a meteor through the dufky air;
His heavenly charms o'ercame her dazled fight,
And drown'd her fenfes in a flood of light;

His

His funny plumes defcending he difplay'd,
And foftly thus addrefs'd the mournful maid:

" Say, thou, who doft yon wondrous ring poffefs,
" What cares difturb thee, or what wants opprefs;
" To faithful ears difclofe thy fecret grief,
" And hope (fo heaven ordains) a quick relief."

The maid replied, " Ah, facred genius, bear
" A hopelefs damfel from this land of care;
" Waft me to fofter climes and lovelier plains,
" Where nature fmiles, and fpring eternal reigns."

She fpoke; and fwifter than the glance of thought
To a fair ifle his fleeping charge he brought.

Now morning breath'd : the fcented air was mild,
Each meadow bloffom'd, and each valley fmil'd;
On every fhrub the pearly dewdrops hung,
On every branch a feather'd warbler fung;
The cheerful fpring her flowery chaplets wove,
And incenfe-breathing gales perfum'd the grove.

                                        The

The damfel rofe; and, loft in glad furprize,
Caft round the gay expanfe her opening eyes,
That fhone with pleafure like a ftarry beam,
Or moonlight fparkling on a filver ftream.
She thought fome nymph muft haunt that lovely fcene,
Some woodland goddefs, or fome fairy queen;
At leaft fhe hop'd in fome fequefter'd vale
To hear the fhepherd tell his amorous tale:
Led by thefe flattering hopes from glade to glade,
From lawn to lawn with hafty fteps fhe ftray'd;
But not a nymph by ftream or fountain ftood,
And not a fairy glided through the wood;
No damfel wanton'd o'er the dewy flowers,
No fhepherd fung beneath the rofy bowers:
On every fide fhe faw vaft mountains rife,
That thruft their daring foreheads in the fkies;
The rocks of polifh'd alabafter feem'd,
And in the fun their lofty fummits gleam'd.
She call'd aloud, but not a voice replied,
Save echo babling from the mountain's fide,

By

By this had night o'ercaſt the gloomy ſcene,
And twinkling ſtars emblaz'd the blue ſerene
Yet on ſhe wander'd till with grief oppreſt
She fell; and, falling, ſmote her ſnowy breaſt:
Now to the heavens her guilty head ſhe rears,
And pours her burſting ſorrow into tears;
Then plaintive ſpeaks, " Ah! fond miſtaken maid,
" How was thy mind by gilded hopes betray'd!
" Why didſt thou wiſh for bowers and flowery hills,
" For ſmiling meadows, and for purling rills;
" Since on thoſe hills no youth or damſel roves,
" No ſhepherd haunts the ſolitary groves?
" Ye meads that glow with intermingled dyes,
" Ye flowering palms that from yon hillocks riſe,
" Ye quivering brooks that ſoftly murmur by,
" Ye panting gales that on the branches die;
" Ah! why has Nature through her gay domain
" Diſplay'd your beauties, yet diſplay'd in vain?
" In vain, ye flowers, you boaſt your vernal bloom,
" And waſte in barren air your freſh perfume,
" Ah! leave, ye wanton birds, yon lonely ſpray;
" Unheard you warble, and unſeen you play:

" Yet

" Yet ftay till fate has fix'd my early doom,
" And ftrow with leaves a haplefs damfel's tomb.
" Some grot or graffy bank fhall be my bier,
" My maiden herfe unwater'd with a tear."

Thus while fhe mourns, o'erwhelm'd in deep defpair,
She rends her filken robes, and golden hair:
Her fatal ring, the caufe of all her woes,
On a hard rock with maddening rage fhe throws;
The gem, rebounding from the ftone, difplays
Its verdant hue, and fheds refrefhing rays:
Sudden defcends the genius of the ring,
And drops celeftial fragrance from his wing;
Then fpeaks, " Who calls me from the realms of day?
" Afk, and I grant; command, and I obey."

She drank his melting words with ravifh'd ears,
And ftopp'd the gufhing current of her tears;
Then kifs'd his fkirts, that like a ruby glow'd,
And faid, " O bear me to my fire's abode."

Straight o'er her eyes a fhady veil arofe,
And all her foul was lull'd in ftill repofe.

By

By this with flowers the rofy-finger'd dawn
Had fpread each dewy hill and verdurous lawn ;
She wak'd, and faw a new-built tomb that ftood
In the dark bofom of a folemn wood,
While thefe fad founds her trembling ears invade :
" Beneath yon marble fleeps thy father's fhade."
She figh'd, fhe wept ; fhe ftruck her penfive breaft,
And bade his urn in peaceful flumber reft.

And now in filence o'er the gloomy land
She faw advance a flowly-winding band ;
Their cheeks were veil'd, their robes of mournful hue
Flow'd o'er the lawn, and fwept the pearly dew ;
O'er the frefh turf they fprinkled fweet perfume,
And ftrow'd with flowers the venerable tomb.
A graceful matron walk'd before the train,
And tun'd in notes of wo the funeral ftrain :
When from her face her filken veil fhe drew,
The watchful maid her aged mother knew.
O'erpowered with burfting joy fhe runs to meet
The mourning dame, and falls before her feet.
The matron with furprize her daughter rears,
Hangs on her neck, and mingles tears with tears.

Now

Now o'er the tomb their hallow'd rites they pay,
And form with lamps an artificial day:
Erelong the damfel reach'd her native vale,
And told with joyful heart her moral tale;
Refign'd to heaven, and loft to all befide,
She liv'd contented, and contented died.

THE

THE

SEVEN FOUNTAINS,

AN EASTERN ALLEGORY.

Written in the Year 1767.

D ECK'D with fresh garlands, like a rural bride,
  And with the crimson streamer's waving pride,
A wanton bark was floating o'er the main,
And seem'd with scorn to view the azure plain:
Smooth were the waves; and scarce a whispering gale
Fann'd with his gentle plumes the silken sail.
High on the burnish'd deck, a gilded throne
With orient pearls and beaming diamonds shone;

D · On

On which reclin'd a youth of graceful mien,
His fandals purple, and his mantle green;
His locks in ringlets o'er his fhoulders roll'd,
And on his cheek appear'd the downy gold.
Around him ftood a train of fmiling boys,
Sporting with idle cheer and mirthful toys;
* Ten comely ftriplings, girt with fpangled wings,
Blew piercing flutes, or touch'd the quivering ftrings;
Ten more, in cadence to the fprightly ftrain,
Wak'd with their golden oars the flumbering main:
The waters yielded to their guiltlefs blows,
And the green billows fparkled as they rofe.

Long time the barge had danc'd along the deep,
And on its glaffy bofom feem'd to fleep;
† But now a glittering ifle arofe in view,
Bounded with hillocks of a verdant hue:
Frefh groves and rofeate bowers appear'd above,
(Fit haunts, be fure, of pleafure and of love)
And higher ftill a thoufand blazing fpires
Seem'd with gilt tops to threat the heavenly fires.
Now each fair ftripling plied his labouring oar,
And ftraight the pinnace ftruck the fandy fhore.

* The follies of youth   † The world.

The

The youth arofe, and, leaping on the ftrand,
.. Took his lone way along the filver fand;
While the light bark, and all the airy crew,
Sunk like a mift beneath the briny dew.

With eager fteps the young adventurer ftray'd
Through many a grove, and many a winding glade:
At length he heard the chime of tuneful ftrings,
That fweetly floated on the Zephyr's wings;
* And foon a band of damfels blithe and fair,
With flowing mantles and difhevel'd hair,
Rufh'd with quick pace along the folemn wood,
Where rapt in wonder and delight he ftood:
In loofe tranfparent robes they were array'd,
Which half their beauties hid, and half difplay'd.

A lovely nymph approach'd him with a fmile,
And faid, " O, welcome to this blifsful ifle!
·· " For thou art he, whom ancient bards foretold,
" Doom'd in our clime to bring an age of gold:
" Hail, facred king! and from thy fubject's hand,
" Accept the robes and fceptre of the land."

* The follies and vanities of the world.

" Sweet

" Sweet maid, faid he, fair learning's heavenly beam
" O'er my young mind n'er fhed her favouring gleam;
" Nor has my arm e'er hurl'd the fatal lance,
" While defperate legions o'er the plain advance.
" How fhould a fimple youth, unfit to bear
" The fteely mail, that fplendid mantle wear!"
" Ah! faid the damfel, from this happy fhore,
" We banifh wifdom, and her idle lore;
" No clarions here the ftrains of battle fing,
" With notes of mirth our joyful valleys ring.
" Peace to the brave! o'er us the beauteous reign,
" And ever-charming pleafures form our train."

This faid, a diadem, inlay'd with pearls,
She plac'd refpectful on his golden curls;
Another o'er his graceful fhoulder threw
A filken mantle of the rofe's hue,
Which, clafp'd with ftuds of gold, behind him flow'd,
And through the folds his glowing bofom fhow'd.
Then in a car, by fnow-white courfers drawn,
They led him o'er the dew-befprinkled lawn,
Through groves of joy and arbours of delight,
With all that could allure his ravifh'd fight;

Green

Green hillocks, meads, and rofy grots, he view'd,
And verdurous plains with winding ftreams bedew'd.
On every bank, and under every fhade,
A thoufand youths, a thoufand damfels play'd;
Some wantonly were tripping in a ring
On the foft border of a gufhing fpring;
While fome, reclining in the fhady vales,
Told to their fmiling loves their amorous tales :
But when the fportful train beheld from far
The nymphs returning with the ftately car,
O'er the fmooth plain with hafty fteps they came,
And hail'd their youthful king with loud acclaim;
With flowers of every tint the paths they ftrow'd,
And caft their chaplets on the hallow'd road.

At laft they reach'd the bofom of a wood,
Where on a hill a radiant palace ftood;
A fumptuous dome, by hands immortal made,
Which on its walls and on its gates difplay'd
The gems that in the rocks of Tibet glow,
The pearls that in the fhells of Ormus grow.
And now a numerous train advance to meet
The youth, defcending from his regal feat;

Whom

Whom to a rich and fpacious hall they led,
With filken carpets delicately fpread :
There on a throne, with gems unnumber'd grac'd,
Their lovely king fix blooming damfels plac'd *,
And, meekly kneeling, to his modeft hand
They gave the glittering fceptre of command;
Then on fix fmaller thrones they fat reclin'd,
And watch'd the rifing tranfports of his mind :
When thus the youth a blufhing nymph addrefs'd,
And, as he fpoke, her hand with rapture prefs'd ;

" Say, gentle damfel, may I afk unblam'd,
" How this gay ifle, and fplendid feats are nam'd ?
" And you, fair queens of beauty and of grace,
" Are you of earthly or celeftial race ?
" To me the world's bright treafures were unknown,
" Where late I wander'd, penfive and alone;
" And, flowly winding on my native fhore,
" Saw the vaft ocean roll, but faw no more;
" Till from the waves with many a charming fong,
" A barge arofe, and gayly mov'd along;
" The jolly rowers reach'd the yielding fands,
" Allur'd my fteps, and wav'd their fhining hands :

* The pleafures of the fenfes.

" I went,

" I went, faluted by the vocal train,
" And the fwift pinnace cleav'd the waves again;
" When on this ifland ftruck the gilded prow,
" I landed full of joy : the reft you know.
" Short is the ftory of my tender years : ..
" Now fpeak, fweet nymph, and charm my liftening
  " cars."

" Thefe are the groves, for ever deck'd with flowers,
" The maid replied, and thefe the fragrant bowers,
" Where Love and Pleafure hold their airy court,
" The feat of blifs, of fprightlinefs, and fport;
" And we, dear youth, are nymphs of heavenly line;
" Our fouls immortal, as our forms divine :
" For Maia, fill'd with Zephyr's warm embrace,
" In caves and forefts cover'd her difgrace ;
" At laft fhe refted on this peaceful fhore,
" Where in yon grot a lovely boy fhe bore,
" Whom frefh and wild and frolick from his birth
" She nurs'd in myrtle bowers, and call'd him Mirth.
" He on a fummer's morning chanc'd to rove
" Through the green labyrinth of fome fhady grove,
" Where, by a dimpled rivulet's verdant fide,
" A rifing bank, with woodbine edg'd, he fpied :

D 4   " There,

" There, veil'd with flowerets of a thoufand hues,

" A nymph lay bath'd in flumber's balmy dews;

" (This maid by fome, for fome our race defame,

" Was Folly call'd, but Pleafure was her name:)

" Her mantle, like the fky in April, blue,

" Hung on a bloffom'd branch that near her grew;

" For, long difporting in the filver ftream,

" She fhunn'd the blazing day-ftar's fultry beam;

" And, ere fhe could conceal her naked charms,

" Sleep caught her trembling in his downy arms:

" Borne on the wings of Love, he flew, and prefs'd

" Her breathing bofom to his eager breaft,

" At his wild theft the rofy morning blufh'd,

" The rivulet fmil'd, and all the woods were hufh'd,

" Of thefe fair parents on this blifsful coaft

" (Parents like Mirth and Pleafure who can boaft?)

" I with five fifters, on one happy morn,

" All fair alike, behold us now, were born.

" When they to brighter regions took their way,

" By Love invited to the realms of day,

" To us they gave this large, this gay domain,

" And faid, departing, Here let Beauty reign.

" Then reign, fair prince, in thee all beauties fhine,

" And, ah! we know thee of no mortal line."

                                    She

She faid; the king with rapid ardour glow'd,
And the fwift poifon through his bofom flow'd:
But while fhe fpoke he caft his eyes around
To view the dazzling roof, and fpangled ground;
Then, turning with amaze from fide to fide,
Seven golden doors, that richly fhone, he fpied,
And faid, "Fair nymph, (but let me not be bold)
"What mean thofe doors that blaze with burnifh'd
    "gold?"
"To fix gay bowers, the maid replied, they lead,
"Where Spring eternal crowns the glowing mead;
"Six fountains there, that glitter as they play,
"Rife to the fun with many a colour'd ray."
"But the feventh door, faid he, what beauties grace!"
"O, 'tis a cave, a dark and joylefs place,
"A fcene of namelefs deeds, and magick fpells,
"Where day ne'er fhines, and pleafure never dwells:
"Think not of that.   But come, my royal friend,
"And fee what joys thy favour'd fteps attend."
She fpoke, and pointed to the neareft door:
Swift he defcends; the damfel flies before;
She turns the lock; it opens at command;
The maid and ftripling enter hand in hand.

                                    The

The wondering youth beheld an opening glade,
Where in the midft a cryftal fountain play'd * ;
The filver fands, that on its bottom grew,
Were ftrown with pearls and gems of varied hue ;
The diamond fparkled like the ftar of day,
And the foft topaz fhed a golden ray ;
Clear amethyfts combin'd their purple gleam
With the mild emerald's fight-refrefhing beam ;
The fapphire fmil'd like yon blue plain above,
And rubies fpread the blufhing tint of love.
" Thefe are the waters of eternal light,
" The damfel faid, the ftream of heavenly fight ;
" See, in this cup (fhe fpoke, and ftoop'd to fill
" A vafe of jafper with the facred rill),
" See, how the living waters bound and fhine,
" Which this well-polifh'd gem can fcarce confine !"
From her foft hand the lucid urn he took,
And quaff'd the nectar with a tender look :
Straight from his eyes a cloud of darknefs flew,
And all the fcene was open'd to his view ;
Not all the groves, where ancient bards have told,
Of vegetable gems, and blooming gold;

* Sight.

Not

Not all the bowers which oft in flowery lays
And folemn tales Arabian poets praife;
Though ftreams of honey flow'd through every mead,
Though balm and amber dropp'd from every reed;
Held half the fweets that Nature's ample hand
Had pour'd luxuriant o'er this wondrous land.
All flowerets here their mingled rays diffufe,
The rainbow's tints to thefe were vulgar hues;
All birds that in the ftream their pinion dip,
Or from the brink the liquid cryftal fip,
Or fhow their beauties to the funny fkies,
Here wav'd their plumes that fhone with varying dyes;
But chiefly he, that o'er the verdant plain
Spreads the gay eyes which grace his fpangled train;
And he, who, proudly failing, loves to fhow
His mantling wings and neck of downy fnow;
Nor abfent he, who learns the human found,
With wavy gold and moving emeralds crown'd;
Whofe head and breaft with polifh'd fapphires glow,
And on whofe wing the gems of Indus grow.
The monarch view'd their beauties o'er and o'er,
He was all eye, and look'd from every pore.
But now the damfel calls him from his trance;
And o'er the lawn delighted they advance:

They

They pafs the hall adorn'd with royal ftate,
And enter now with joy the fecond gate *.

  A foothing found he heard, (but tafted firft
The gufhing ftream that from the valley burft),
And in the fhade beheld a youthful quire
That touch'd with flying hands the trembling lyre:
Melodious notes, drawn out with magick art,
Caught with fweet extafy his ravifh'd heart;
An hundred nymphs their charming defcants play'd,
And melting voices died along the glade;
The tuneful ftream that murmur'd as it rofe,
The birds that on the trees bewail'd their woes,
The boughs, made vocal by the whifpering gale,
Join'd their foft ftrain, and warbled through the vale.
The concert ends: and now the ftripling hears
A tender voice that ftrikes his wondering ears;
A beauteous bird, in our rude climes unknown,
That on a leafy arbour fits alone,
Strains his fweet throat, and waves his purple wings,
And thus in human accents foftly fings:

       * Hearing.

                                    " Rife,

" Rife, lovely pair, a fweeter bower invites
" Your eager fteps, a bower of new delights;
" Ah! crop the flowers of pleafure while they blow,
" Ere winter hides them in a veil of fnow.
" Youth, like a thin anemone, difplays
" His filken leaf, and in a morn decays.
" See, gentle youth, a lily-bofom'd bride!
" See, nymph, a blooming ftripling by thy fide!
" Then hafte, and bathe your fouls in foft delights,
" A fweeter bow'r your wandering fteps invites."

He ceas'd; the flender branch, from which he flew,
Bent its fair head, and fprinkled pearly dew.
The damfel fmil'd; the blufhing youth was pleas'd,
And by her willing hand his charmer feiz'd:
The lovely nymph, who figh'd for fweeter joy,
To the third gate * conducts the amorous boy;
She turns the key; her cheeks like rofes bloom,
And on the lock her fingers drop perfume.

His ravifh'd fenfe a fcene of pleafure meets,
A maze of joy, a paradife of fweets;

* Smell.

But

But firſt his lips had touch'd th' alluring ſtream,
That through the grove diſplay'd a ſilver gleam.
Through jaſmine bowers, and violet-ſcented vales,
On ſilken pinions flew the wanton gales,
Arabian odours on the plants they left,
And whiſper'd to the woods their ſpicy theft;
Beneath the ſhrubs, that ſpread a trembling ſhade,
The muſky roes, and fragrant civets, play'd.
As when at eve an Eaſtern merchant roves
From Hadramut to Aden's ſpikenard groves,
Where ſome rich caravan not long before
Has paſs'd, with caſſia fraught, and balmy ſtore,
Charm'd with the ſcent that hills and vales diffuſe,
His grateful journey gayly he purſues;
Thus pleas'd, the monarch fed his eager ſoul,
And from each breeze a cloud of fragrance ſtole :
Soon the fourth door * he paſs'd with eager haſte,
And the fourth ſtream was nectar to his taſte.

Before his eyes, on agate columns rear'd,
On high a purple canopy appear'd;
And under it in ſtately form was plac'd
A table with a thouſand vaſes grac'd;

* Taſte.

Laden

Laden with all the dainties that are found
In air, in feas, or on the fruitful ground.
Here the fair youth reclin'd with decent pride,
His wanton nymph was feated by his fide :
All that could pleafe the tafte the happy pair
Cull'd from the loaded board with curious care;
O'er their enchanted heads a mantling vine
His curling tendrils wove with amorous twine;
From the green ftalks the glowing clufters hung
Like rubies on a thread of emeralds ftrung;
With thefe were other fruits of every hue,
The pale, the red, the golden, and the blue.
An hundred fmiling pages ftood around,
Their fhining brows with wreaths of myrtle bound :
They, in tranfparent cups of agate, bore
Of fweetly-fparkling wines a precious ftore ;
The ftripling fipp'd and revel'd, till the fun
Down heaven's blue vault his daily courfe had run;
Then rofe, and, follow'd by the gentle maid,
Op'd the fifth door * : a ftream before them play'd.

The king, impatient for the cooling draught,
In a full cup the myftic nectar quaff'd;

* Touch.

Then

Then with a ſmile (he knew no higher bliſs)
From her ſweet lip he ſtole a balmy kiſs:
On the ſmooth bank of violets they reclin'd;
And, whilſt a chaplet for his brow ſhe twin'd,
With his ſoft cheek her ſofter cheek he preſs'd,
His pliant arms were folded round her breaſt.
She ſmil'd, ſoft lightning darted from her eyes,
And from his fragrant ſeat ſhe bade him riſe;
Then, while a brighter bluſh her face o'erſpread,
To the ſixth gate * her willing gueſt ſhe led.

The golden lock ſhe ſoftly turn'd around;
The moving hinges gave a pleaſing ſound:
The boy delighted ran with eager haſte,
And to his lips the living fountain plac'd;
The magick water pierc'd his kindled brain,
And a ſtrange venom ſhot from vein to vein.
Whatever charms he ſaw in other bowers,
Were here combin'd, fruits, muſick, odours, flowers;
A couch beſides, with ſofteſt ſilk o'erlaid;
And, ſweeter ſtill, a lovely yielding maid,
Who now more charming ſeem'd, and not ſo coy,
And in her arms infolds the bluſhing boy:

* The ſenſual pleaſures united.

They

They fport and wanton, till, with fleep opprefs'd,
Like two frefh rofe-buds on one ftalk, they reft.

When morning fpread around her purple flame,
To the fweet couch the five fair fifters came;
They hail'd the bridegroom with a cheerful voice,
And bade him make with fpeed a fecond choice.
Hard tafk to choofe, when all alike were fair!
Now this, now that, engag'd his anxious care:
Then to the firft who fpoke his hand he lent;
The reft retir'd, and whifper'd as they went.
The prince enamour'd view'd his fecond bride;
They left the bower, and wander'd fide by fide;
With her he charm'd his ears, with her his fight;
With her he pafs'd the day, with her the night.
Thus all by turns the fprightly ftranger led,
And all by turns partook his nuptial bed;
Hours, days, and months, in pleafure flow'd away;
All laugh'd, all fweetly fung, and all were gay.

So had he wanton'd threefcore days and feven,
More bleft, he thought, than any fon of heaven:
Till on a morn, with fighs and ftreaming tears,
The train of nymphs before his bed appears;

E   And

And thus the youngeſt of the ſiſters ſpeaks,
Whilſt a ſad ſhower runs trickling down her cheeks:

" A cuſtom which we cannot, dare not fail,
" (Such are the laws that in our iſle prevail)
" Compels us, prince, to leave thee here alone,
" Till thrice the ſun his riſing front has ſhown:
" Our parents, whom, alas! we muſt obey,
" Expect us at a ſplendid feaſt to-day;
" What joy to us can all their ſplendour give?
" With thee, with only thee, we wiſh to live.
" Yet may we hope, theſe gardens will afford
" Some pleaſing ſolace to our abſent lord?
" Six golden keys, that ope yon bliſsful gates,
" Where joy, eternal joy, thy ſteps awaits,
" Accept: the ſeventh (but that you heard before)
" Leads to a cave, where ravening monſters roar;
" A ſullen, dire, inhoſpitable cell,
" Where deathful ſpirits and magicians dwell.
" Farewel, dear youth; how will our boſoms burn
" For the ſweet moment of our bleſt return!"

The king, who wept, yet knew his tears were vain,
Took the ſeven keys, and kiſs'd the parting train.

                              A glit-

A glittering car, which bounding courfers drew,
They mounted ftraight, and through the foreft flew.

The youth, unknowing how to pafs the day,
Review'd the bowers, and heard the fountains play;
By hands unfeen whate'er he wifh'd was brought;
And pleafures rofe obedient to his thought.
Yet all the fweets, that ravifh'd him before,
Were tedious now, and charm'd his foul no more:
Lefs lovely ftill, and ftill lefs gay they grew;
He figh'd, he wifh'd, and long'd for fomething new:
Back to the hall he turn'd his weary feet,
And fat repining on his royal feat:
Now on the feventh bright gate he cafts his eyes
And in his bofom rofe a bold furmife:
" The nymph, faid he, was fure difpos'd to jeft;
" Who talk'd of dungeons in a place fo bleft:
" What harm to open, if it be a cell
" Where deathful fpirits and magicians dwell?
" If dark or foul, I need not pafs the door;
" If new or ftrange, my foul defires no more."
He faid, and rofe; then took the golden keys,
And op'd the door: the hinges mov'd with eafe:

E 2   Before

Before his eyes appear'd a fullen gloom,
Thick, hideous, wild; a cavern, or a tomb.
Yet as he longer gaz'd, he faw afar
A light that fparkled like a fhooting ftar.
He paus'd: at laft, by fome kind angel led,
He enter'd, and advanc'd with cautious tread.
Still as he walk'd, the light appear'd more clear;
Hope.footh'd him then, and fcarcely left a fear.
At length an aged fire furpriz'd he faw,
Who fill'd his bofom with a facred awe *:
A book he held, which, as reclin'd he lay,
He read, affifted by a taper's ray;
His beard, more white than fnow on winter's breaft,
Hung to the zone that bound his fable veft;
A pleafing calmnefs on his brow was feen,
Mild was his look, majeftick was his mien.
Soon as the youth approach'd the reverend fage,
He rais'd his head, and clos'd the ferious page;
Then fpoke: " O fon, what chance has turn'd thy feet
" To this dull folitude, and lone retreat?"
To whom the youth: " Firft, holy father, tell,
" What force detains thee in this gloomy cell?

* Religion.

" This

" This ifle, this palace, and thofe balmy bowers,
" Where fix fweet fountains fall on living flowers,
" Are mine; a train of damfels chofe me king,
" And through my kingdom fmiles perpetual fpring.
" For fome important caufe to me unknown,
" This day they left me joylefs and alone;
" But, ere three morns with rofes ftrow the fkies,
" My lovely brides will charm my longing eyes."

" Youth, faid the fire, on this aufpicious day
" Some angel hither led thy erring way :
" Hear a ftrange tale, and tremble at the fnare,
" Which for thy fteps thy pleafing foes prepare.
" Know, in this ifle prevails a bloody law;
" Lift, ftripling, lift! (the youth ftood fix'd with awe :)
" * But feventy days the haplefs monarchs reign,
" Then clofe their lives in exile and in pain;
" Doom'd in a deep and frightful cave to rove,
" Where darknefs hovers o'er the iron grove.
" Yet know, thy prudence and thy timely care
" May fave thee, fon, from this deftructive fnare.
" † Not far from this a lovelier ifland lies,
" Too rich, too fplendid, for unhallow'd eyes:

* The life of man. † Heaven.

" On

" On that bleſt ſhore a ſweeter fountain flows
" Than this vain clime, or this gay palace knows,
" Which if thou taſte, whate'er was ſweet before
" Will bitter ſeem, and ſteal thy ſoul no more.
" But, ere theſe happy waters thou canſt reach,
" Thy weary ſteps muſt paſs yon rugged beech,
" * Where the dark ſea with angry billows raves,
" And, fraught with monſters, curls his howling waves;
" If to my words obedient thou attend,
" Behold in me thy pilot and thy friend.
" A bark I keep, ſupplied with plenteous ſtore,
" That now lies anchor'd on the rocky ſhore;
" And, when of all thy regal toys bereft,
" In the rude cave an exile thou art left,
" Myſelf will find thee on the gloomy lea,
" And waft thee ſafely o'er the dangerous ſea."

The boy was fill'd with wonder as he ſpake,
And from a dream of folly ſeem'd to wake:
All day the ſage his tainted thoughts refin'd;
His reaſon brighten'd, and reform'd his mind:
Through the dim cavern hand in hand they walk'd,
And much of truth, and much of heaven, they talk'd.

* Death.

At

At night the ftripling to the hall return'd;
With other fires his alter'd bofom burn'd.
O ! to his wifer foul how low, how mean,
Seem'd all he e'er had heard, had felt, had feen !
He view'd the ftars, he view'd the cryftal fkies,
And blefs'd the power all-good, all-great, all-wife;
How lowly now appear'd the purple robe,
The rubied fceptre, and the ivory globe !
How dim the rays that gild the brittle earth !
How vile the brood of Folly, and of Mirth !

When the third morning, clad in mantle gray,
Brought in her rofy car the feventieth day,
A band of flaves, who rufh'd with furious found,
In chains of fteel the willing captive bound;
From his young head the diadem they tore,
And caft his pearly bracelets on the floor;
They rent his robe that bore the rofe's hue,
And o'er his breaft a hairy mantle threw;
Then dragg'd him to the damp and dreary cave,
Drench'd by the gloomy fea's refounding wave.
Meanwhile the voices of a numerous croud
Pierc'd the dun air, as thunder breaks a cloud:

The

The nymphs another haplefs youth had found,
And then were leading o'er the guilty ground :
They hail'd him king (alas, how fhort his reign!)
And with frefh chaplets ftrow'd the fatal plain,

The happy exile, monarch now no more,
Was roving flowly o'er the lonely fhore ;
At laft the fire's expected voice he knew,
And tow'rd the found with hafty rapture flew.
The promis'd pinnace juft afloat he found,
And the glad fage his fetter'd hands unbound ;
But when he faw the foaming billows rave,
And dragons rolling o'er the fiery wave,
He ftopp'd : his guardian caught his lingering hand,
And gently led him o'er the rocky ftrand ;
Soon as he touch'd the bark, the ocean fmil'd,
The dragons vanifh'd, and the waves were mild.

For many an hour with vigorous arms they row'd,
While not a ftar one friendly fparkle fhow'd ;
At length a glimmering brightnefs they behold,
Like a thin cloud which morning dyes with gold :
To that they fteer ; and now, rejoic'd, they view
A fhore begirt with cliffs of radiant hue.

The

They land : a train, in fhining mantles clad,
Hail their approach, and bid the youth be glad;
They led him o'er the lea with eafy pace,
And floated as they went with heavenly grace.
A golden fountain foon appear'd in fight,
That o'er the border caft a funny light.

   The fage, impatient, fcoop'd the lucid wave
In a rich vafe, which to the youth he gave;
He drank : and ftraight a bright celeftial beam
Before his eyes difplay'd a dazzling gleam ;
Myriads of airy fhapes around him gaz'd ;
Some prais'd his wifdom, fome his courage prais'd;
Then o'er his limbs a ftarry robe they fpread,
And plac'd a crown of diamonds on his head.

   His aged guide was gone, and in his place
Stood a fair cherub flufh'd with rofy grace ;
Who, fmiling, fpake: " Here ever wilt thou reft,
" Admir'd, belov'd, our brother and our gueft;
" So all fhall end, whom vice can charm no more
" With the gay follies of that perilous fhore.
" See yon immortal towers their gates unfold,
" With rubies flaming, and no earthly gold !

                             " There

" There joys, before unknown, thy fteps invite ;

" Blifs without care, and morn without a night.

" But now farewel ! my duty calls me hence ;

" Some injur'd mortal afks my juft defence.

" To yon pernicious ifland I repair,

" Swift as a ftar." He fpeaks, and melts in air.

The youth o'er walks of jafper takes his flight;

And bounds and blazes in eternal light.

A PER-

A PERSIAN SONG

OF HAFIZ.

SWEET maid, if thou would'st charm my fight,
  And bid thefe arms thy neck infold;
That rofy cheek, that lily hand,
Would give thy poet more delight
Than all Bocara's vaunted gold,
Than all the gems of Samarcand.

GAZEL.

EGHER an Turki Shirazi
  Bedeft ared dili mara,
Be khali hinduifh bakhfhem
  Samarcand u Bokharara.

آن ترک شیرازی

بست آرد دل مرا

کی هندویش بینشم

رقند و بخـــارا

Boy,

Boy, let yon liquid ruby flow,

And bid thy penfive heart be glad,

Whate'er the frowning zealots fay :

Tell them, their Eden cannot fhow

A ftream fo clear as Rocnabad,

A bower fo fweet as Mofellay.

O ! when thefe fair perfidious maids,

Whofe eyes our fecret haunts infeft,

Their dear deftructive charms difplay ;

Each glance my tender breaft invades,

And robs my wounded foul of reft,

As Tartars feize their deftin'd prey,

Bedeh, faki, mei baki,

     Ke der jennet nekhahi yaft

Kunari abi Rocnabad,

     Ve gulgefhti Mofellara.

Fugan kein luliani fhokh

     I fhiringari fhehrafhob

Chunan berdendi fabr az dil

     Ke Turcan khani yagmara.

In

In vain with love our bofoms glow :
Can all our tears, can all our fighs,
New luftre to thofe charms impart ?
Can cheeks, where living rofes blow,
Where nature fpreads her richeft dyes,
Require the borrow'd glofs of art ?

Speak not of fate :—ah ! change the theme,
And talk of odours, talk of wine,
Talk of the flowers that round us bloom :
'Tis all a cloud, 'tis all a dream ;
To love and joy thy thoughts confine,
Nor hope to pierce the facred gloom.

Ze efhki na temami ma
    Jamali yari muftagnift ;
Be ab u reng u khal u khatt
    Che hajet ruyi zibara.

Hadis az mutreb u mei gu,
    Va razi dehri kemter ju,
Ke kes nekfhud u nekfhaied
    Be hikmet ein moammara.

Beauty

Beauty has fuch refiftlefs power,
That even the chafte Egyptian dame
Sigh'd for the blooming Hebrew boy;
For her how fatal was the hour,
When to the banks of Nilus came
A youth fo lovely and fo coy!

But ah! fweet maid, my counfel hear
(Youth fhould attend when thofe advife
Whom long experience renders fage):
While mufick charms the ravifh'd ear;
While fparkling cups delight our eyes,
Be gay; and fcorn the frowns of age.

Men az an hufni ruzafzun
     Ke Yufuf dafhti daneftem
Ke efhk az perdei ifmet
     Berun ared Zuleikhara.

Nafihet gofhi kun jana,
     Ke az jan doftiter darend
Juvanani faadetmend
     I pendi peeri danara.

What

What cruel anſwer have I heard!
And yet, by heaven, I love thee ſtill:
Can aught be cruel from thy lip?
Yet ſay, how fell that bitter word
From lips which ſtreams of ſweetneſs fill,
Which nought but drops of honey ſip?

Go boldly forth, my ſimple lay,
Whoſe accents flow with artleſs eaſe,
Like orient pearls at random ſtrung:
Thy notes are ſweet, the damſels ſay;
But O! far ſweeter, if they pleaſe
The nymph for whom theſe notes are ſung.

Bedem gufti, va khurſendam,
    Afac alla, neku gufti,
Jawabi telkhi mizeibed
    Lebi lali ſheker khara.

Gazel gufti vedurr ſufti,
    Bea vakhoſh bukhan Hafiz,
Ke ber nazmi to afſhaned
    Felek ikdi ſuriara.

A N

✳✳✳✳✳✳✳✳✳✳✳✳✳✳✳✳✳✳✳✳✳✳✳✳✳ ✳

A N

ODE OF PETRARCH,

TO THE

FOUNTAIN OF VALCHIUSA.

Y E clear and sparkling streams,
  Warm'd by the funny beams;
Through whose transparent crystal Laura play'd;
  Ye boughs, that deck the grove,
  Where Spring her chaplets wove,
While Laura lay beneath the quivering shade;

Canzone 27.

Chiare, fresche, e dolci acque,
Ove le belle membra
Pose colei, che sola a me par donna;
Gentil ramo, ove piacque
(Con sospir mi rimembra)
A lei di fare al bel fianco colonna;

* M. de Voltaire has given us a beautiful paraphrase of this first
stanza, though it is certain that he had never read the ode in the ori-

F   ginal,

Sweet herbs, and blushing flowers,
That crown yon vernal bowers
For ever fatal, yet for ever dear;
 And ye, that heard my sighs
 When first she charm'd my eyes,
Soft-breathing gales, my dying accents hear.

Erba, e fior', che la gonna
Leggiadra ricoverse
Coll' angelico seno;
Aer facro fereno
Ov' Amor co' begli occhi il cor m' aperfe;
Date udiénza infieme
Alle dolenti mie parole eftreme.

ginal, or at moft only the three firft lines of it; for he afferts that the
Italian fong is irregular, and without rhymes; whereas the ftanzas
are perfectly regular, and the rhymes very exact. His defign was to
give Madame du Châtelet, for whom he wrote his hiftory, an idea
of Petrarch's ftyle; but, if fhe had only read his imitation, fhe could
have but an imperfect notion of the Italian, which the reader will
eafily perceive by comparing them.

If

If heaven has fix'd my doom,
That Love muſt quite confume
My burſting heart, and cloſe my eyes in death;
Ah! grant this ſlight requeſt,
That here my urn may reſt
When to its manſion flies my vital breath;
This pleaſing hope will ſmooth
My anxious mind, and ſooth
The pangs of that inevitable hour;
My ſpirit will not grieve
Her mortal veil to leave
In theſe calm ſhades, and this enchanting bower.

S' egli è pur mio deſtino,
E'l cielo in ciò s' adopra,
Ch' amor queſti occhi lagrimando chiuda;
Qualche grazia il meſchino
Corpo fra voi ricopra;
E torni l' alma al proprio albergo ignuda:
La morte fia men cruda,
Se queſta ſpeme porto
A quel dubbioſo paſſo;
Che lo ſpirito laſſo
Non poria mai in piu ripoſato porto
N'en piu tranquilla foſſa
Fuggir la carne travagliata, e l' oſſa.

Haply

Haply the guilty maid
Through yon accuftom'd glade
To my fad tomb.will take her lonely way;
Where firft her beauty's light,
O'erpower'd my dazzled fight,
When Love on this fair border bade me ftray:
There forrowing fhall fhe fee,
Beneath an aged tree,
Her true but haplefs lover's lowly bier;
Too late her tender fighs.
Shall melt the pitying fkies,
And her foft veil fhall hide the gufhing tear.

Tempo verrà ancor forfe
Ch' all' ufato foggiorno
Torni la fera bella e manfueta;
E là, ov' ella mi fcorfe
Nel benedetto giorno
Volga la vifta defiofa e lieta,
Cercandomi, ed, o pieta,
Già terra infra le pietre
Vedendo, Amor l'infpiri
In guifa che fofpiri
Si dolcemente che mercè m'impetre,
E faccia forza al cielo
Afciugandofi gli occhi col bel velo.

OL

O ! well-remember'd day,

When on yon bank fhe lay,

Meek in her pride, and in her rigour mild;

The young and blooming flowers,

Falling in fragrant fhowers,

Shone on her neck, and on her bofom fmil'd:

Some on her mantle hung,

Some in her locks were ftrung,

Like orient gems in rings of flaming gold;

Some, in a fpicy cloud

Defcending, call'd aloud,

" Here Love and Youth the reins of empire hold."

Da' bei rami fcendea

Dolce nella memoria

Una pioggia di fior fovra 'l fuo grembo;

Ed ella fi fedea,

Humile in tanta gloria

Coverta già dell' amorofo nembo:

Qual fior cadea ful lembo,

Qual fulle treccie bionde,

Ch' oro forbito e perle

Eran quel di a vederle,

Qual fi pofava in terra, e qual full' onde;

Qual con un vago errore

Girando parea dir, " Qui regna Amore."

I view'd

I view'd the heavenly maid;
And, rapt in wonder, faid
" The groves of Eden gave this angel birth;"
Her look, her voice, her fmile,
That might all heaven beguile,
Wafted my foul above the realms of earth :
The ftar-befpangled fkies
Were open'd to my eyes;
Sighing I faid, " Whence rofe this glittering fcene ?"
Since that aufpicious hour,
This bank, and odorous bower,
My morning couch, and evening haunt, have been.

Quante volte difs'io
Allor pien di fpavento
" Coftei per fermo nacque in paradifo,"
Cofi carco d' oblio
Il divin portamento
E'l volto, e le parole, e'l dolce rifo
M' avenno, e fi divifo
Dall' imagine vera,
Ch' i' dicea fofpirando,
" Qui come venn' io, o quando ?"
Credendo effer' in ciel, non là dov' era.
Da indi in quà mi piace
Quefta erba fi ch' altrove non o pace.

Well

Well mayſt thou bluſh, my ſong,
To leave the rural throng,
And fly thus artleſs to my Laura's ear;
But, were thy poet's fire
Ardent as his deſire,
Thou wert a ſong that heaven might ſtoop to hear.

Se tu aveſſi órnamenti quant' ai voglia,
Potreíti arditamente
Uſcir del boſco, e gir' infra la gente.

M. DE VOLTAIRE's PARAPHRASE

OF THE

FIRST STANZA,

Chiare, frefche, e dolci acque &c.

CLAIRE fontaine, onde aimable, onde pure,
 Ou la beauté qui confume mon cœur,
Seule beauté, qui foit dans la nature,
Des feux du jour evite la chaleur;
  Arbre heureux, dont le feuillage
  · Agité par les Zephirs
  La couvris de fon ombrage,
  Qui rappelles mes foupirs,
  En rappellant fon image,

Ornemens

Ornemens de ces bords, et filles du matin,

Vous dont je fuis jaloux, vous moins brillantes qu'Elle,

Fleurs, qu'elle embelliſſait, quand vous touchiez ſon ſein, ·

Roſſignols, dont la voix eſt moins douce et moins belle, ·'

Air devenu plus pur, adorable ſéjour,

      Immortaliſé par ſes charmes,

Lieux dangereux et chers, ou de ſes tendres armes

      L'amour a bleſſé tous mes ſens,

      Ecoutez mes derniers accens,

      Recevez mes dernieres larmes.

L A U R A,

L A U R A,

An ELEGY from PETRARCH.

*IN this fair feafon, when the whifpering gales
    Drop fhowers of fragrance o'er the bloomy vales,
From bower to bower the vernal warblers play;
The fkies are cloudlefs, and the meads are gay;

IMITATIONS.
  * Ver. 1. Petrarch. Sonnet. 270.
Zefiro torna, e'l bel tempo rimena,
    E' i fiori, e l' erbe, fua dolce famiglia;
    E garrir Progne, e pianger Filomela;
    E primavera candida, e vermiglia:

                          Ridozo

The nightingale in many a melting ſtrain

Sings to the groves, " Here Mirth and Beauty reign."

But me, for ever bath'd in guſhing tears,

No mirth enlivens, and no beauty cheers :

The birds that warble, and the flowers that bloom,

Relieve no more this ſolitary gloom.

I ſee, where late the verdant meadow ſmil'd,

A joyleſs deſert, and a dreary wild.

For thoſe dear eyes, that pierc'd my heart before,

Are clos'd in death, and charm the world no more ;

IMITATIONS,

Ridono i prati, e'l ciel ſi raſſerena;

　　Giove s'allegra di mirar ſua figlia;

　　L'aria, e l'acque, e la terra è d'amor piena;

　　Ogni animal d'amar ſi riconſiglia :

Ma per me, laſſo, tornano i piu gravi

　　Soſpiri, che del cor profondo tragge

　　Quella ch' al ciel ſe ne portò le chiavi :

E cantar' augelletti, e fiorir piagge,

　　E'n belle donne oneſte atti ſoavi,

　　Sono un deſerto, e fere aſpre e ſelvagge.

Loft

Loſt are thoſe treſſes, that outſhone the morn,
And pale thoſe cheeks, that might the ſkies adorn.
* Ah, death! thy hand has cropp'd the faireſt flower,
That ſhed its ſmiling rays in beauty's bower;
Thy dart has lay'd on yonder ſable bier
All my ſoul lov'd, and all the world held dear;
Celeſtial ſweetneſs, love-inſpiring youth,
Soft-ey'd benevolence, and white-rob'd truth.

    † Hard fate of man, on whom the heavens beſtow
A drop of pleaſure for a ſea of woe!

IMITATIONS.

* Ver. 17. Sonnet. 243.

Diſcolorato ai, morte, il piu bel volto
    Che mai ſi vede, e'i plu begli oechi ſpenti;
    Spirto piu acceſo di virtuti ardenti
    Del piu leggiadro, e piu bel nodo ai ſciolto!

† Ver. 28. Sonnet, 230.

O noſtra vita, ch'è ſi bella in viſta!
    Com' perde agevolmente in un' mattina
    Quel che'n molt' anni a gran pena s' acquiſta.

Ah,

Ah, life of care, in fears or hopes confum'd,
Vain hopes, that wither ere they well have bloom'd!
How oft, emerging from the fhades of night,
Laughs the gay morn, and fpreads a purple light;
But foon the gathering clouds o'erfhade the fkies,
Red lightnings play, and thundering ftorms arife!
How oft a day, that fair and mild appears,
Grows dark with fate, and mars the toil of years!

* Not far remov'd, yet hid from diftant eyes,
Low in her fecret grot a Naiad lies.

I M I T A T I O N S.

* Ver. 33. See a defcription of this celebrated fountain in a
poem of Madame Defhoulieres.

Entre de hauts rochers, dont l'afpect eft terrible,
Des pres toujours fleuris, des arbres toujours verds,
　　Une fource orgueilleufe et pure,
　　Dont l' eau fur cent rochers divers
　　D' une mouffe verte couverts,
　　S' épanche, bouillonne, et murmure;
Des agneaux bondiffans fur la tendre verdure,
Et de leurs conducteurs les ruftiques concerts, &c.

　　　　　　　　　　　　　　Steep

Steep arching rocks, with verdant moſs o'ergrown,
Form her rude diadem, and native throne :
There in a gloomy cave her waters ſleep,
Clear as a brook, but as an ocean deep.
Yet, when the waking flowers of April blow,
And warmer ſunbeams melt the gather'd ſnow;
Rich with the tribute of the vernal rains,
The nymph, exulting, burſts her ſilver chains;
Her living waves in ſparkling columns riſe,
And ſhine like rainbows to the ſunny ſkies;
From cliff to cliff the falling waters roar;
Then die in murmurs, and are heard no more.
Hence, ſoftly flowing in a dimpled ſtream,
The cryſtal Sorga ſpreads a lively gleam;
From which a thouſand rills in mazes glide,
And deck the banks with ſummer's gayeſt pride;
Brighten the verdure of the ſmiling plains,
And crown the labour of the joyful ſwains.

Firſt on theſe banks (ah, dream of ſhort delight !)
The charms of Laura ſtruck my dazzled ſight;
Charms, that the bliſs of Eden might reſtore,
That heaven might envy, and mankind adore.

I ſaw—

I faw—and O ! what heart could long rebel ?
I faw, I lov'd, and bade the world farewel.
Where'er fhe mov'd, the meads were frefh and gay;
And every bower exhal'd the fweets of May ;
Smooth flow'd the ftreams, and foftly blew the gale ;
The rifing flowers impurpled every dale ;
Calm was the ocean, and the fky ferene ;
An univerfal fmile o'erfpread the fhining fcene :
But when in death's cold arms entranc'd fhe lay,
(* Ah, ever dear, yet ever fatal day !)
O'er all the air a direful gloom was fpread ;
Pale were the meads, and all their bloffoms dead ;
The clouds of April fhed a baleful dew,
All nature wore a veil of deadly hue.

Go, plaintive breeze, to Laura's flowery bier,
Heave the warm figh, and fhed the tender tear.
There to the awful fhade due homage pay,
And foftly thus addrefs the facred clay :

* Laura was firft feen by Petrarch on the fixth of April in the
year 1327; and fhe died on the fame day in 1348.

* Say

" * Say, envied earth, that doſt thoſe charms infold,

" Where are thoſe cheeks, and where thoſe locks of gold?

" Where are thoſe eyes, which oft the Muſe has ſung?

" Where thoſe ſweet lips, and that enchanting tongue?

" Ye radiant treſſes, and thou, nectar'd ſmile;

" Ye looks that might the melting ſkies beguile;

" You robb'd my ſoul of reſt, my eyes of ſleep;

" You taught me how to love, and how to weep."

I M I T A T I O N S.

* Ver. 75. Sonnet. 260.

Quanta invidia ti porto, avara terra,
Ch' abbracci quella, cui veder m' è tolto;

And Sonnet. 259.

Ov' è la fronte, che con picciol cenno
    Volgea 'l mio core in queſta parte, e'n quella?
    Ov' è 'l bel ciglio, e l' una e l' altra ſtella,
    Ch' al corſo del mio viver lume denno? &c.

G   No

* No ſhrub o'erhangs the dew-beſpangled vale,
No bloſſom trembles to the dying gale,
No floweret bluſhes in the morning rays,
No ſtream along the winding valley plays,
But knows what anguiſh thrills my tortur'd breaſt,
What pains conſume me, and what cares infeſt.
* At bluſh of dawn, and in the gloom of night,
Her pale-eyed phantom ſwims before my ſight,

IMITATIONS.

* Ver. 83. Sonnet. 248.

Non è ſterpe, ne ſaſſo in queſti monti,
   Non ramo o fronda verde in queſte piagge;
   Non fior' in queſte valli, o foglia d'erba;
Stilla d' acque non' ven di queſte fonti,
   Ne fiere an queſti boſchi ſi ſelvagge,
   Che non ſappian quant' è mia pena acerba.

      † Ver. 89. Sonnet. 241.

Or' in forma di ninfa, o d' altra diva,
   Che del piu chiaro fondo di Sorga eſca,
   E pongaſi a ſeder' in ſu la riva:
Or' i' o veduta ſu per l'erba freſca
   Calcar' i fior, com' una donna viva,
   Moſtrando in viſta, che di me le'ncreſca.

                              Sits

Sits on the border of each purling rill,
Crowns every bower, and glides o'er every hill.
* Flows the loud rivulet down the mountain's brow?
Or pants the Zephyr on the waving bough?
Or fips the labouring bee her balmy dews,
And with foft ftrains her fragrant toil purfues?
Or warbles from yon filver-bloffom'd thorn
The wakeful bird, that hails the rifing morn?

IMITATIONS.

* Ver. 93. Sonnet. 239.

Se lamentar' augelli, o verdi fronde
   Mover foavemente all' aura eftiva,
   O roco mormorar di lucid' onde
S'ode d'una fiorita e frefca riva,
La v' io feggia d' amor penfofo, e fchriva;
   Lei che'l ciel ne moftrò, terra nafconde,
   Veggio, ed odo, ed intendo, ch' ancor viva
Di fi lontano a' fofpir miei rifponde.
Deh! perche innanzi tempo ti confume?
   Mi dice con pietate, a che pur verfi
   Dagli occhi trifti un dolorofo fiume?
Di me non pianger tu; che miei di ferfi,
   Morendo, eterni, e nell' eterno lume,
   Quando moftrai di chiuder gl' occhi, aperfi.

My

My Laura's voice in many a foothing note
Floats through the yielding air, or feems to float:

" Why fill thy fighs, fhe fays, this lonely bower ?
" Why down thy bofom flows this endlefs fhower ?
" Complain no more ; but hope ere long to meet
" Thy much-loy'd Laura in a happier feat.
" Here fairer fcenes detain my parted fhade ;
" Suns that ne'er fet, and flowers that never fade :
" Through cryftal fkies I wing my joyous flight,
" And revel in eternal blaze of light ;
" See all thy wanderings in that vale of tears,
" And fmile at all thy hopes, at all thy fears :
" Death wak'd my foul, that flept in life before,
" And op'd thefe brighten'd eyes, to fleep no more."

She ends : the fates, that will no more reveal,
Fix on her clofing lips their facred feal.
" Return, fweet fhade ! I wake, and fondly fay,
" O, cheer my gloom with one far-beaming ray !
" Return : thy charms my forrow will difpel,
" And fnatch my fpirit from her mortal cell ;
" Then, mix'd with thine, exulting fhe fhall fly,
" And bound enrap'tur'd through her native fky."

She

She comes no more : my pangs more fierce return ;
Tears gufh in ftreams, and fighs my bofom burn.
* Ye banks, that oft my weary limbs have born;
Ye murmuring brooks, that learnt of me to mourn ; ·
Ye birds, that tune with me your plaintive lay ;
Ye groves, where Love once taught my fteps to ftray;
You, ever fweet and ever fair, renew
Your ftrains melodious, and your blooming hue ;
But not in my fad heart can blifs remain,
My heart, the haunt of never-ceafing pain !

I M I T A T I O N S.

* Ver. 123. Sonnet. 261.

Valle, che de' lamenti miei fe' piena;
    Fiume, che fpeffo del mio pianger crefci ;
    Fere felveftre, vaghi augelli, e pefci,
    Che l' una, e l' altra verde riva affrena;
Aria de' miei folpir' calda e ferena;
    Dolce fentier, che fi amaro riefci ; ·
    Colle, che mi piacefti, or mi rincrefci ;
    Ov' ancor per ufanza Amor mi mena ;
Ben riconofco in voi l'ufate forme,
    Non, laffo, in me, che da fi lieta vifta,
    Son fatto albergo d'infinita doglia.

Henceforth, to fing in fmoothly-warbled lays
The fmiles of youth, and beauty's heavenly rays;
* To fee the morn her early charms unfold,
Her cheeks of rofes, and her curls of gold;
† Led by the facred Mufe at noon to rove
O'er tufted mountain, vale, or fhady grove;

IMITATIONS.

* Ver. 133. Sonnet. 251.

Quand' io veggio dal ciel fcender l'Aurora,
   Con la fronte di rofe, e co' crin d' oro,

† Ver. 135. Sonnet. 272.

Ne per fereno ciel ir vaghe ftelle;
   Ne per tranquillo mar legni fpalmati;
   Ne per campagne cavalieri armati;
   Ne per bei bofchi allegre fere e fnelle;
Ne d' afpettato ben frefche novelle,
   Ne dir d'Amore in ftili alti ed ornati;
   Ne tra chiare fontane, e verdi prati
   Dolce cantare onefte donne e belle;
Ne altro farà mai ch' al cor m' aggiunga,
   Si feco il feppe quella fepellire,
   Che fola a gli occhi miei fu lume e fpeglio,

To

To watch the ftars, that gild the lucid pole,
And view yon orbs in mazy order roll;
To hear the tender nightingale complain,
And warble to the woods her amorous ftrain;
No more fhall thefe my penfive foul delight,
But each gay vifion melts in endlefs night.

* Nymphs, who in·glimmering glades by moonlight
  dance,
And ye, who through the liquid cryftal glance,
Who oft have heard my fadly-pleafing moan;
Behold me now a lifelefs marble grown.
Ah! lead me to the tomb where Laura lies;
Clouds, fold me round; and, gather'd darknefs, rife;
Bear me, ye gales, in death's foft flumber lay'd;
And, ye bright realms, receive my fleeting fhade!

I M I T A T I O N S.

* Ver. 143. Sonnet. 263.

O vaghi abitator de' verdi bofchi,
  O Ninfe, e voi, che'l frefco erbofo fondo
  Del liquido criftallo·alberga e pafce.

A T U R-

A

TURKISH ODE

OF MESIHI.

HEAR how the nightingales, on every spray,
Hail in wild notes the sweet return of May!
The gale, that o'er yon waving almond blows,
The verdant bank with silver bloffoms ftrows:
The fmiling feafon decks each flowery glade.
Be gay: too foon the flowers of Spring will fade.

DINLEH bulbul kiffa fen kim gildi eiami behar,
Kurdi her bir baghda hengamei hengami behar,
Oldi fim affhan ana ezhari badami behar
Yfh u nufh it kim gicher kalmaz bu eiami behar.

*Thou heareft the tale of the nightingale, " that the vernal feafon
" approaches." The Spring has fpread a bower of joy in every grove,
where the almond-tree fheds its filver bloffoms. Be cheerful; be full
of mirth; for the Spring paffes foon away: it will not laft.*

What

What gales of fragrance fcent the vernal air!
Hills, dales, and woods, their lovelieft mantles wear,
Who knows what cares await that fatal day,
When ruder gufts fhall banifh gentle May?
Ev'n death, perhaps, our valleys will invade.
Be gay: too foon the flowers of Spring will fade.

The tulip now its varied hue difplays,
And fheds, like Ahmed's eye, celeftial rays.
Ah, nation ever faithful, ever true,
The joys of youth, while May invites, purfue!
Will not thefe notes your timorous minds perfuade?
Be gay: too foon the flowers of Spring will fade.

Yineh enwei fhukufileh bezendi bagh u ragh,
Yfh ichun kurdi chichekler fahni gulfhenda otagh,
Kim bilur ol behareh dek kih u kim ola fagh?
Yfh u nufh it kim gicher kahnaz bu ciami behar,

Tarafi gulfhen nuri Ahmed birleh malamaldur,
Sebzelerinda fehabeh lalehi kheirulaldur,
Hei Mohammed ummeti wakti huzuri haldur,
Yfh u nufh it kim gicher kalmaz bu eiami behar,

*The groves and hills are again adorned with all forts of flowers:
a pavilion of rofes, as the feat of pleafure, is raifed in the garden.
Who knows which of us will be alive when the fair feafon enas?
Be cheerful, &c.*

*The edge of the bower is filled with the light of Ahmed: among
the plants the fortunate tulips reprefent his companions. Come,
O people of Mohammed, this is the feafon of merriment. Be
cheerful, &c.*

The

The fparkling dewdrops o'er the lilies play,
Like orient pearls, or like the beams of day. •
If love and mirth your wanton thoughts engage,
Attend, ye nymphs! (a poet's words are fage).
While thus you fit beneath the trembling fhade,
Be gay: too foon the flowers of Spring will fade.

The frefh blown rofe like Zeineb's cheek appears,
When pearls, like dewdrops, glitter in her ears.
The charms of youth at once are feen and paft;
And nature fays, " They are too fweet to laft."
So blooms the rofe; and fo the blufhing maid!
Be gay: too foon the flowers of Spring will fade.

Kildi fhebnem yineh jeuherdari tighi fufeni,
Zhalehler aldi hewai doiyile leh gulfhene, •
Gher temafha ifeh makfudun beni efleh beni.
Yfh u nufh it kim gicher kalmaz bu eiami behar.
Rukhleri rengin'giuzellär dur gulileh lalehlar,
Kim kulaklarineh durlu jeuher afmifh zhalehlar,
Aldanup fonma ki bunlar boileh baki kalehlar.
Yfh u nufh it kim gicher kalmaz bu eiami behar.

*Again the dew glitters on the leaves of the lily, like the water of
a bright fcymitar. The dewdrops fall through the air on the garden
of rofes. Liften to me, liften to me, if thou defireft to be delighted.
Be cheerful, &c.*

*The rofes and tulips are like the bright cheeks of beautiful maids,
in whofe ears the pearls hang like drops of dew. Deceive not thyfelf,
by thinking that thefe charms will have a long duration. Be cheerful, &c.*

See

See yon anemonies their leaves unfold,
With rubies flaming, and with living gold !
While cryſtal ſhowers from weeping clouds deſcend,
Enjoy the preſence of thy tuneful friend.
Now, while the wines are brought, the ſofa's lay'd,
Be gay : too ſoon the flowers of Spring will fade.

The plants no more are dried, the meadows dead,
No more the roſe-bud hangs her penſive head :
The ſhrubs revive in valleys, meads, and bowers,
And every ſtalk is diadem'd with flowers;
In ſilken robes each hillock ſtands array'd.
Be gay : too ſoon the flowers of Spring will fade.

Guliſtanda giorunin laleh u gul naoman leh
Baghda kan aldi ſhemſun niſhteri baran leh,
Arefun bu demi khoſh gior bu giun yaran leh,
Yſh u nuſh it kim gicher kalmaz bu eiami behar,

Gitti ol demler ki olup ſebzeler ſahib feraſh,
Guncheh fikri gulſhenun olmiſhdi bagherinda baſh,
Gildi bir dem kim karardi laleh lerle dagh u taſh,
Yſh u nuſh it kim gicher kalmaz bu eiami behar.

Tulips, roſes, and anemonies, appear in the gardens: the ſhowers and the ſunbeams, like ſharp lancets, tinge the banks with the colour of blood. Spend this day agreeably with thy friends, like a prudent man. Be cheerful, &c.

The time is paſſed in which the plants were ſick, and the roſe-bud hung its thoughtful head on its boſom. The ſeaſon comes in which mountains and rocks are coloured with tulips. Be cheerful, &c.

Clear

Clear drops each morn impearl the rofe's bloom,
And from its leaf the Zephyr drinks perfume;
The dewy buds expand their lucid ftore :
Be this our wealth : ye damfels, afk no more.
Though wife men envy, and though fools upbraid,
Be gay : too foon the flowers of Spring will fade.

The dewdrops, fprinkled by the mufky gale,
Are chang'd to effence ere they reach the dale.
The mild blue fky a rich pavilion fpreads,
Without our labour, o'er our favour'd heads.
Let others toil in war, in arts, or trade.
Be gay : too foon the flowers of Spring will fade.

Ebr gulzari uftuneh her fubh goher bariken,
Nefhei badi feher por nafei tatariken :
Ghafil olmeh alemun mahbublighi wariken.
Yfh u nufh it kim gicher kalmaz bu eiami behar.

Buyi gulzar itti fholdenlu hewai mufhknab
Kim yereh inengeh olur ketrei fhebnem gulab.
Cherkh otak kurdi guliftan uftuneh giunlik fehab.
Yfh u nufh it kim gicher kalmaz bu eiami behar.

Each morning the clouds fhed gems over the rofe-garden : the breath of the gale is full of Tartarian mufk. Be not neglectful of thy duty through too great a love of the world. Be cheerful, &c.

The fweetnefs of the bower has made the air fo fragrant, that the dew, before it falls, is changed into rofe-water. The fky fpreads a pavilion of bright clouds over the garden. Be cheerful, &c.

Let

Late gloomy winter chill'd the fullen air,
Till Soliman arofe, and all was fair.
Soft in his reign the notes of love refound,
And pleafure's rofy cup goes freely round.
Here on the bank, which mantling vines o'erfhade,
Be gay : too foon the flowers of Spring will fade.

May this rude lay from age to age remain,
A true memorial of this lovely train.
Come, charming maid, and hear thy poet fing,
Thyfelf the rofe, and He the bird of fpring :
Love bids him fing, and Love will be obey'd.
Be gay : too foon the flowers of Spring will fade.

Guliftanun her ne fen aldi fiah badi khuzan,
Adl idup bir bir ileh wardi yineh fhahi jehan.
Deuletinda badehler kam oldi fakii kamran.
Yfh u nufh it kim gicher kalmaz bu eiami behar.

Omerem bulch, Mefihi, bu merbai ifhtihar,
Ehlene ola bu charabru u giuzeller yadgar,
Bulbuli khofh gui fen gulyuzluler leh yuriwar.
Yfh u nufh it kim gicher kalmaz bu eiami behar.

Whoever thou art, know that the black gufts of autumn had feized the garden; but the king of the world again appeared difpenfing juftice to all: in his reign the happy cupbearer defired and obtained the flowing wine. Be cheerful, &c.

By thefe ftrains I hoped to celebrate this delightful valley: may they be a memorial to its inhabitants, and remind them of this affembly, and thefe fair maias! Thou art a nightingale with a fweet voice, O Mefihi, when thou walkeft with the damfels, whofe cheeks are like rofes. Be cheerful; be full of mirth; for the Spring paffes foon away: it will not laft.

THE

THE SAME,

PERVIGILIUM VENERIS.

ALITES audis loquaces per nemora, per arbutos,
  Veris adventum canentes tinnulo modulamine;
Dulcè luget per virentes mollis aura amygdalas :
Nunc amandum eſt, nunc bibendum; floreum ver fugit,
  abit !

Ecce jam flores refulgent gemmeis honoribus,
Quique prata, quique ſaltûs, quique ſylvulas amant;
Quis ſcit an nox una nobis dormienda æterna ſit ?
Nunc amandum eſt, nunc bibendum; floreum ver fugit,
  abit !

Quantus eſt nitor roſarum ! quantus hyacinthi decor !
Non ocellus, cùm renidet, eſt puellæ lætior :
Hic levi dies amori eſt, hic voluptati ſacer :
Nunc amandum eſt, nunc bibendum; floreum ver fugit,
  abit !

Ecce

Ecce baccatæ recentis guttulæ roris micant,
Per genam rofæ cadentes, perque mite lilium:
Auribus gratum, puellæ, fit meum veftris melos;
Nunc amandum eft, nunc bibendum; floreum ver fugit,
 'abit !

Ut rofa in prato refulget, fic teres virgo nitet,
Hæc onufta margaritis, illa roris gemmulis:
Ne perenne vel puellæ vel rofæ fperes decus.
Nunc amandum eft, nunc bibendum; floreum ver fugit,
 abit !

Afpice, ut rofeta amictu difcolori fplendeant,
Prata dum frœcundat æther læta gratis imbribus,
Fervidos inter fodales da voluptati diem.
Nunc amandum eft, nunc bibendum; floreum ver fugit,
 abit !

Jam fitu deformis ægro non jacet rofæ calyx;
Ver adeft, ver pingit hortos purpurantes floribus,
Perque faxa, perque colles, perque lucos emicat:
Nunc amandum eft, nunc bibendum; floreum ver fugit,
 abit l

                                        Ecce,

Ecce, per rofæ papillas fuavè rident guttulae,
Quas odorifer refolvit lenis aurae fpiritus;
Hae pyropis, hae fmaragdis cariores Indicis.
Nunc amandum eft, nunc bibendum; floreum ver fugit,
    abit!

Is tenellis per vireta fpirat è rofis odor,
Ut novum ftillans amomum ros in herbas decidat,
Suavè olentibus coronans lacrymis conopeum.
Nunc amandum eft, nunc bibendum; floreum ver fugit,
    abit!

Acris olim cum malignis faeviit ventis hyems;
Sed rofeto, folis inftar, regis affulfit nitor;
Floruit nemus repentè, dulce manavit merum:
Nunc amandum eft, nunc bibendum; floreum ver fugit,
    abit!

His iners modis, Mefihi, melleam aptabas chelyn;
Veris ales eft poeta; verna cantat gaudia,
Et rofas carpit tepentes è puellarum genis.
Nunc amandum eft, nunc bibendum; floreum ver fugit,
    abit!

ARCADIA,

ARCADIA,

A PASTORAL POEM.

ADVERTISEMENT.

THE following paſtoral was written in the year 1762; but the author, finding ſome tolerable paſſages in it, was induced to correct it afterwards, and to give it a place in this collection. He took the hint of it from an allegory of Mr. Addiſon, in the thirty-ſecond paper of the Guardian; which is •ſet down in the margin, that the reader may ſee where he has copied the original, and where he has deviated from it. In this piece, as it now ſtands, Menalcas, king of the ſhepherds, means Theocritus, the moſt ancient,

H   and

and perhaps the beft, writer of paftorals : and by his two daughters, Daphne and Hyla, muft be underftood the two forts of paftoral poetry; the one elegant and polifhed, the other fimple and unadorned; in both of which he excelled. Virgil, whom Pope chiefly followed, feems to have borne away the palm in the higher fort; and Spenfer, whom Gay imitated with fuccefs, had equal merit in the more ruftick ftyle : thefe two poets, therefore, may juftly be fuppofed in this allegory to have inherited his kingdom of Arcadia.

ARCADIA.

A   R   C   A   D   I   A.

I N thofe fair plains, where glittering Ladon roll'd
His wanton labyrinth o'er fands of gold,
Menalcas reign'd : from Pan his lineage came ;
Rich were his vales, and deathlefs was his fame.
When youth impell'd him, and when love infpir'd,
The liftening nymphs his Dorick lays admir'd :

IMITATIONS.

Guardian, N° 32.

In ancient times there dwelt in a pleafant vale of Arcadia a
man of very ample poffeffions, named Menalcas, who, deriving
his pedigree from the god Pan, kept very ftrictly up to the rules
of the paftoral life, as it was in the golden age.

H 2   To

To hear his notes the fwains with rapture flew;
A fofter pipe no fhepherd ever blew.
But now, opprefs'd beneath the load of age,
Belov'd, refpcted, venerable, fage,
* Of heroes, demigods, and gods he fung;
His reed neglected on a poplar hung:
Yet all the rules, that young Arcadians keep,
He kept, and watch'd each morn his bleating fheep.

Two lovely daughters were his deareft care;
Both mild as May, and both as April fair:
Love, where they mov'd, each youthful breaft inflam'd;
And Daphne this, and Hyla that was nam'd.
† The firft was bafhful as a blooming bride,
And all her mien difplay'd a decent pride;

I M I T A T I O N S.

† He had a daughter, his only child, called Amaryllis. She was a virgin of a moft enchanting beauty, of a moft eafy and unaffected air; but, having been bred up wholly in the country, was bafhful to the laft degree.

N O T E.

* This couplet alludes to the higher Idyllia of Theocritus; as the Ἐγκώμιον εἰς Πτολμαῖον, the Διόσκυροι, and others, which are of the heroic kind.

Her

Her treſſes, braided in a curious knot,
Were cloſe confin'd, and not a hair forgot;
Where many a flower, in myſtick order plac'd,
With myrtle twin'd, her ſilken fillet grac'd;
Nor with leſs neatneſs was her robe diſpos'd,
And every fold a pleaſing art diſclos'd;
Her ſandals of the brighteſt ſilk were made,
And, as ſhe walk'd, gave luſtre to the ſhade;
A graceful eaſe in every ſtep was ſeen,
She mov'd a ſhepherdeſs, yet look'd a queen.
Her ſiſter ſcorn'd to dwell in arching bowers,
Or deck her locks with wreaths of fading flowers;
O'er her bare ſhoulder flow'd her auburn hair,
And, fann'd by Zephyrs, floated on the air;
Green were her buſkins, green the veſt ſhe wore,
And in her hand a knotty crook ſhe bore.
* The voice of Daphne might all pains diſarm;
Yet, heard too long, its ſweetneſs ceas'd to charm:

IMITATIONS.

* She had a voice that was exceedingly ſwcet; yet had a
ruſticity in her tone, which, however, to moſt who heard her
ſeemed an additional charm. Though in her converſation in
general ſhe was very engaging, yet to her lovers, who were

But none were tir'd when artlefs Hyla fung,
Though fomething ruftick warbled from her tongue.

Thus both in beauty grew, and both in fame,
Their manners different, yet their charms the fame,
The young Arcadians, tuneful from their birth,
To love devoted, and to rural mirth,
Beheld, and fondly lov'd the royal maids,
And fung their praife in valleys, lawns, and glades;
From morn to lateft eve they wept, and figh'd;
And fome for Daphne, fome for Hyla, died:
Each day new prefents to the nymphs they bore,
And in gay order fpread the fhining ftore;
Some beechen bowls and polifh'd fheephooks brought,
With ebon knots, and ftuds of filver, wrought;
Some led in flowery bands the playful fawn,
Or bounding roe, that fpurn'd the graffy lawn;
The reft on nature's blooming gifts relied,
And rais'd their flender hopes on beauty's pride:

IMITATIONS.

numerous, fhe was fo coy, that many left her in difguft after a
tedious courtfhip, and matched themfelves where they were
better received.

But

But the coy maids, regardlefs of their pain,
Their vows derided, and their plaintive ftrain.
Hence fome, whom love with lighter flames had fir'd,
Broke their foft flutes, and in defpair retir'd;
To milder damfels told their amorous tale, ·
And found a kinder Daphne in the vale.

It happen'd on a cheerful morn of May,
When every meadow fmil'd in frefh array,
The fhepherds, rifing at an early hour,
In crouds affembled round the regal bower,
There hail'd in fprightly notes the peerlefs maids;
And tender accents trembled through the glades.
Menalcas, whom the larks with many a lay
Had call'd from flumber at the dawn of day,
By chance was roving through a bordering dale,
And heard the fwains their youthful woes bewail.
He knew the caufe; for long his prudent mind
To footh their cares indulgently defign'd:
Slow he approach'd; then wav'd his awful hand,
And, leaning on his crook, addrefs'd the liftening band.

" Arcadian fhepherds, to my words attend!
In filence hear your monarch, and your friend.

H 4   Your

Your fruitlefs pains, which none can difapprove,
Excite my pity, not my anger move.
Two gentle maids, the folace of my age,.
Fill all my foul, and all my care engage;
When death fhall join me to the pale-ey'd throng,
To them my fylvan empire will belong;
But, left with them the royal line fhould fail,
And civil difcord fill this happy vale,
Two chofen youths the beauteous nymphs muft wed,
To fhare their power, and grace the genial bed:
* So may the fwains our ancient laws obey,
And all Arcadia own their potent fway.
But what fage counfel can their choice direct?
Whom can the nymphs prefer, or whom reject?
So like your paffion, and fo like your ftrain,
That all deferve, yet cannot all obtain.

IMITATIONS.

* For Menalcas had not only refolved to take a fon-in-law, who fhould inviolably maintain the cuftoms of his family; but had received one evening, as he walked in the fields, a pipe of an antique form from a Faun, or, as fome fay, from Oberon the Fairy, with a particular charge, not to beftow his daughter on any one who could not play the fame tune upon it as at that time he entertained him with,

So

Hear then my tale : as late, by fancy led
To steep Cyllene's ever-vocal head,
With winding steps I wander'd through the wood,
And pour'd wild notes, a Faun before me stood;
A flute he held, which as he softly blew,
The feather'd warblers to the found he drew;
Then to my hand the precious gift confign'd,
And faid, " Menalcas, eafe thy wondering mind :
" This pipe, on which the god of fhepherds play'd,
" When love inflam'd him, and the * viewlefs maid,
" Receive : ev'n Pan thy tuneful fkill confefs'd,
" And after Pan thy lips will grace it beft.
" Thy daughter's beauty every breaft infpires,
" And all thy kingdom glows with equal fires :
" But let thofe favour'd youths alone fucceed,
" Who blow with matchlefs art this heavenly reed."
† This faid, he difappear'd.   Then hear my will :
Be bold, ye lovers, and exert your fkill ;

I M I T A T I O N S.

† When the time that he defigned to give her in marriage
was near at hand, he publifhed a decree, whereby he invited

N O T E.
* Echo.

the

Be they my fons, who fing the fofteft ftrains,
And tune to fweeteft notes their pleafing pains :
But mark ! whoe'er fhall by too harfh a lay
Offend our ears, and from our manners ftray,
He, for our favour, and our throne unfit,
To fome difgraceful penance muft fubmit."

He ends ; the fhepherds at his words rejoice,
And praife their fovereign with a grateful voice.
Each fwain believes the lovely prize his own,
And fits triumphant on th' ideal throne ;
Kind Vanity their want of art fupplies,
And gives indulgent what the Mufe denies ;
Gay vefts and flowery garlands each prepares,
And each the drefs, that fuits his fancy, wears.

IMITATIONS.

the neighbouring youths to make trial of this mufical inftrument, with promife, that the victor fhould poffefs his daughter
on condition that the vanquifhed fhould fubmit to what punifh-
ment he thought fit to inflict. Thofe, who were not yet dif-
couraged, and had high conceits of their own worth, appeared
on the appointed day, in a drefs and equipage fuitable to their
refpective

Now deeper blufhes ting'd the glowing fky,
And evening rais'd her filver lamp on high;
When, in a bower by Ladon's lucid ftream,
Where not a ftar could dart his piercing beam,
So thick the curling eglantines difplay'd,
With woodbines join'd, an aromatick fhade,
The father of the blooming nymphs reclin'd,
His hoary locks with facred laurel twin'd :
The royal damfels, feated by his fide,
Shone like two flowers in fummer's faireft pride ;
The fwains before them crouded in a ring,
Prepar'd to blow the flute, or fweetly fing.

Firft, in the midft a graceful youth arofe,
Born in thofe fields where cryftal Mele flows :

IMITATIONS.

refpective fancies. The place of meeting was a flowery meadow, through which a clear ftream murmured in many irregular meanders. The fhepherds made a fpacious ring for the con-
tending lovers; and in one part of it there fat upon a little
throne of turf, under an arch of eglantine and woodbines, the
father of the maid, and at his right hand the damfel crowned
with rofes and lilies. She wore a flying robe of a flight green
fluff;

His air was courtly, his complexion fair;
And rich perfumes fhed fweetnefs from his hair,
That o'er his fhoulder wav'd in flowing curls,
With rofes braided, and inwreath'd with pearls;
A wand of cedar for his crook he bore;
His flender foot th' Arcadian fandal wore,
Yet that fo rich, it feem'd to fear the ground,
With beaming gems and filken ribbands bound;
The plumage of an oftrich grac'd his head,
And with embroider'd flowers his mantle was o'erfpread.

IMITATIONS.

ftuff; fhe had her fheephook in one hand, and the fatal pipe
in the other. The firft who approached her was a youth of a
graceful prefence and a courtly air, but dreffed in a richer habit
than had ever been feen in Arcadia. He wore a crimfon veft,
cut, indeed, after the fhepherd's fafhion, but fo enriched
with embroidery, and fparkling with jewels, that the eyes of
the fpectators were diverted from confidering the mode of the
garment by the dazzling of the ornaments. His head was co-
vered with a plume of feathers, and his fheephook glittered
with gold and enamel. He applied the pipe to his lips,
and began a tune, which he fet off with fo many graces and
quavers,

* He fung the darling of th' Idalian queen,
Fall'n in his prime on fad Cythera's green;
When weeping graces left the faded plains,
And tun'd their ftrings to elegiack ftrains;
While mourning Loves the tender burden bore,
"Adonis, fair Adonis, charms no more."
The theme difpleas'd the nymph, whofe ruder ear
The tales of fimple fhepherds loy'd to hear.
The maids and youths, who faw the fwain advance,
And take the fatal pipe, prepar'd to dance:
So wildly, fo affectedly, he play'd,
His tune fo various and uncouth he made,
That not a dancer could in cadence move,
And not a nymph the quaver'd notes approve:

I M I T A T I O N S.

quavers, that the fhepherds and fhepherdeffes, who had paired themfelves in order to dance, could not follow it; as indeed it required great fkill and regularity of fteps, which they had never been bred to. Menalcas ordered him to be ftripped of his coftly robes, and to be clad in a ruffet weed, and to tend the flocks in the valleys for a year and a day.

N   O   T   E.

* See Bion, Mofchus, &c.

They

They broke their ranks, and join'd the circling train,.
While burfts of laughter founded o'er the plain.
Menalcas rais'd his hand, and bade retire
The filken courtier from th' Arcadian choir :
Two eager fhepherds, at the king's command,
Rent his gay plume, and fnapp'd his polifh'd wand;
They tore his veft, and o'er his bofom threw
A weed of homely grain and ruffet hue;
Then fill'd with wither'd herbs his fcented locks,
And fcornful drove him to the low-brow'd rocks;
There doom'd to rove, deferted and forlorn,
Till thrice the moon had arch'd her filver horn.

* The next that rofe, and took the myftick reed,
Was wrapp'd ungraceful in a fordid weed:

---

* The fecond that appeared was in a very different garb.
He was cloathed in a garment of rough goat-fkins, his hair was
matted, his beard neglected ; in his perfon uncouth, and awkward
in his gait. He came up fleering to the nymph, and told her,
" He had hugged his lambs, and kiffed his young kids, but he
" hoped to kifs one that was fweeter." The fair one blufhed
with modefty and anger, and prayed fecretly againft him as

A fhaggy hide was o'er his fhoulder fpread,
And wreaths of noxious darnel bound his head;
Unfhorn his beard, and tangled was his hair,
He rudely walk'd, and thus addrefs'd the fair:
" My kids I fondle, and my lambs I kifs;
" Ah! grant, fweet maid, a more delightful blifs."
The damfels blufh with anger and difdain,
And turn indignant from the fhamelefs fwain;
To Pan in filence, and to Love, they pray,
To make his mufick hateful as his lay.
The gods affent: the flute he roughly takes,
And fcarce with pain a grating murmur makes;
But when in jarring notes he forc'd his fong,
Juft indignation fir'd the rural throng:
Shame of Arcadia's bowers! the youths exclaim,
Whofe tunelefs lays difgrace a fhepherd's name!

I M I T A T I O N S.

fhe gave him the pipe. He fnatched it from her, but with
great difficulty made it found; which was in fuch harfh and
jarring notes, that the fhepherds cried one and all that he underftood no mufick. He was immediately ordered to the moft
craggy parts of Arcadia to keep the goats, and commanded
never to touch a pipe any more.

The

The watchful heralds, at Menalcas' nod,
Purfued the ruftick with a vengeful rod ;
Condemn'd three fummers on the rocky fhore
To feed his goats, and touch a pipe no more.

* Now to the ring a portly fwain advanc'd,
Who neither wholly walk'd, nor wholly danc'd ;
Yet mov'd in pain, fo clofe his crimfon veft
Was clafp'd uneafy o'er his ftraining breaft :
† " Fair nymph, faid he, the rofes, which you wear,
" Your charms improve not, but their own impair."

IMITATIONS.

* The third that advanced appeared in clothes that were fo
ftrait and uneafy to him, that he feemed to move in pain. He
marched up to the maiden with a thoughtful look, and ftately
pace, and faid, " Divine Amaryllis, you wear not thofe rofes
" to improve your beauty, but to make them afhamed." As fhe
did not comprehend his meaning, fhe prefented the inftrument
without reply. The tune that he played was fo intricate and
perplexing, that the fhepherds ftood ftill like people aftonifhed
and confounded.

N O T E.

† See Taffo, Guarini, Fontenelle, Camoens, Garci'affo, and Lope
de la Vega ; and other writers of paftorals in Italian, French, Portu-
guefe, and Spanifh.

The

The maids, unus'd to flowers of eloquence,
Smil'd at the words, but could not guefs their fenfe.
When in his hand the facred reed he took,
Long time he view'd it with a penfive look;
Then gave it breath, and rais'd a fhriller note
Than when the bird of morning fwells his throat;
Through every interval, now low, now high,
Swift o'er the ftops his fingers feem'd to fly:
The youths, who heard fuch mufick with furprize,
Gaz'd on the tuneful bard with wondering eyes:
He faw with fecret pride their deep amaze,
Then faid, * "Arcadia fhall refound my praife,
" And every clime my powerful art fhall own;
" This, this, ye fwains, is melody alone:
" To me Amphion taught the heavenly ftrains,
" Amphion, born on rich Hefperian plains."

---

* In vain did he plead that it was the perfection of mufick compofed by the moft fkilful mafter of Hefperia. Menalcas, finding that he was a ftranger, hofpitably took compaffion on him, and delivered him to an old fhepherd, who was ordered to get him clothes that would fit him, and teach him how to fpeak plain.

I   To

To whom Menalcas: " Stranger, we admire
" Thy notes melodious, and thy rapturous fire;
" But ere to thefe fair valleys thou return,
" Adopt our manners, and our language learn:
" Some aged fhepherd fhall thy air improve,
" And teach thee how to fpeak, and how to move."

* Soon to the bower a modeft ftripling came,
Faireft of fwains; and † Tityrus his name:
Mild was his look, an eafy grace he fhow'd,
And o'er his beauteous limbs a decent mantle flow'd:
As through the croud he prefs'd, the fylvan choir
His mien applauded, and his neat attire;
And Daphne, yet untaught in amorous lore,
Felt ftrange defires, and pains unknown before.

I M I T A T I O N S.

* The fourth that ftepped forward was young Amyntas, the
moft beautiful of all the Arcadian fwains, and fecretly beloved
by Amaryllis. He wore that day the fame colours as the maid
for whom he fighed. He moved towards her with an eafy, but
unaffured, air: fhe blufhed as he came near her; and when fhe
gave him the fatal prefent, they both trembled, but neither

N O T E.

† The name fuppofed to be taken by Virgil in his firft paftoral.

could

He now begins; the dancing hills attend,
And knotty oaks from mountain-tops defcend :
He fings of fwains beneath the beechen fhade,
* When lovely Amaryllis fill'd the glade ;
Next, in a fympathizing lay, complains
Of love unpitied, and the lover's pains :
But when with art the hallow'd pipe he blew,
What deep attention hufh'd the rival crew !
He play'd fo fweetly, and fo fweetly fung,
That on each note th' enraptur'd audience hung ;
Ev'n blue-hair'd nymphs, from Ladon's limpid ftream,
Rais'd their bright heads, and liften'd to the theme ;
Then through the yielding waves in tranfport glanc'd;
Whilft on the banks the joyful fhepherds danc'd :

I M I T A T I O N S.

could fpeak. Having fecretly breathed his vows to the gods, he
poured forth fuch melodious notes, that, though they were a
little wild and irregular, they filled every heart with delight.
The fwains immediately mingled in the dance; and the old
fhepherds affirmed, that they had often heard fuch mufick by
night, which they imagined to be played by fome of the rural
deities.

N O T E.

* Formofam refonare doces Amaryllida fylvam. *Virg:*

I 2   " W

" We oft, said they, at close of evening flowers,

" Have heard such musick in the vocal bowers:

" We wonder'd; for we thought some amorous god,

" That on a silver moonbeam swiftly rode,

" Had fann'd with starry plumes the floating air,

" And touch'd his harp, to charm some mortal fair."

He ended; and as rolling billows loud

His praise resounded from the circling croud.

The clamorous tumult softly to compose,

High in the midst the plaintive * Colin rose,

Born on the lilied banks of royal Thame,

Which oft had rung with Rosalinda's name;

Fair, yet neglected; neat, yet unadorn'd;

The pride of dress, and flowers of art, he scorn'd:

And, like the nymph who fir'd his youthful breast,

Green were his buskins, green his simple vest:

With careless ease his rustick lays he sung,

And melody flow'd smoothly from his tongue:

Of June's gay fruits and August's corn he told,

The bloom of April, and December's cold;

N O T E.

* Colin is the name that Spenser takes in his pastorals; and Rosalinda is that under which he celebrates his mistress.

The

* The loves of fhepherds, and their harmlefs cheer

In every month that decks the varied year.

Now on the flute with equal grace he play'd,

And his foft numbers died along the fhade;

The fkilful dancers to his accents mov'd,

And every voice his eafy tune approv'd;

Ev'n Hyla, blooming maid, admir'd the ftrain,

While through her bofom fhot a pleafing pain.

Now all were hufh'd: no rival durft arife;

Pale were their cheeks, and full of tears their eyes.

Menalcas, rifing from his flowery feat,

Thus, with a voice majeftically fweet,

Addrefs'd th' attentive throng: " Arcadians, hear!

" The fky grows dark, and beamy ftars appear:

" Hafte to the vale; the bridal bowers prepare,

" And hail with joy Menalcas' tuneful heir.

" Thou, Tityrus, of fwains the pride and grace,

" Shalt clafp foft Daphne in thy fond embrace:

" And thou, young Colin, in thy willing arms

" Shalt fold my Hyla, fair in native charms

" O'er thefe fweet plains divided empire hold,

" And to your lateft race tranfmit an age of gold.

NOTE.
* See the Shepherd's Kalendar.

I 3 " What

" What fplendid vifions rife before my fight,

" And fill my aged bofom with delight !

" * Henceforth of wars and conqueft fhall you fing,

" Arms and the Man in every clime fhall ring;

" Thy mufe, bold Maro, Tityrus no more,

" Shall tell of chiefs that left the Phrygian fhore,

" Sad Dido's love, and Venus' wandering fon,

" The Latians vanquifh'd, and Lavinia won.

" And thou, O Colin, heaven-defended youth,

" Shalt hide in fiction's veil the charms of truth ;

" Thy notes the fting of forrow fhall beguile,

" And fmooth the brow of anguifh till it fmile ;

" Notes, that a fweet Elyfian dream can raife,

" And lead th' enchanted foul through fancy's maze;

" Thy verfe fhall fhine with Gloriana's name,

" And fill the world with Britain's endlefs fame."

* To Tityrus then he gave the facred flute,
And bade his fons their blufhing brides falute;

IMITATIONS.

* The good old man leaped from his throne, and, after he had embraced him, prefented him to his daughter, which caufed a general acclamation.

N O T E.

* This prophecy of Menalcas alludes to the Æneid of Virgil, and the Fairy-Queen of Spenfer.

Whilft

Whilſt all the train a lay of triumph ſung,
Till mountains echo'd, and till valleys rung.

* While thus with mirth they tun'd the nuptial ſtrain,
A youth, too late, was haſtening o'er the plain,
Clad in a flowing veſt of azure hue;
† Blue were his ſandals, and his girdle blue:
A ſlave, ill-dreſs'd and mean, behind him bore
An oſier-baſket, fill'd with fiſhy ſtore;
The lobſter with his ſable armour bold;
The taſteful mullet deck'd with ſcales of gold;
Bright perch, the tyrants of the finny breed;
And greylings ſweet, that crop the fragrant weed:

IMITATIONS.

* While they were in the midſt of their joy, they were ſur-
priſed with a very odd appearance. A perſon, in a blue mantle, crowned with ſedges and ruſhes, ſtepped into the midſt of
the ring. He had an angling rod in his hand, a pannier upon
his back; and a poor meagre wretch in wet clothes carried ſome
oyſters before him. Being aſked, whence he came, and what

N   O   T   E.

† See Sannazaro, Ongaro, Phineas Fletcher, and other writers of
piſcatory eclogues.

Among them fhells of many a tint appear;

* The heart of Venus, and her pearly ear;

The nautilus, on curling billows born;

And fcallops, by the wandering pilgrim worn;

Some dropp'd with filver, fome with purple dye;

With all the race that feas or ftreams fupply;

A net and angle o'er his fhoulder hung:

Thus was the ftranger clad, and thus he fung:

" Ah! lovely damfel, leave thy fimple fheep;

" 'Tis fweeter in the fea-worn rock to fleep:

" There fhall thy line the fcaly fhoals betray,

" And fports, unknown before, beguile the day;

" To guide o'er rolling waves the dancing fkiff,

" Or pluck the famphire from th' impending cliff:

" My rapturous notes the blue-ey'd Nereids praife,

" And filver-footed Naiads hear my lays."

I M I T A T I O N S,

he was, he told them he was come to invite Amaryllis from the plains to the fea-fhore; that his fubftance confifted in fea-calves; and that he was acquainted with the Nereids and Naiads. " Art thou acquainted with the Naiads?" faid Menal-cas, " to them fhalt thou return." The fhepherds immediately hoifted him up as an enemy to Arcadia, and plunged him in the river, where he funk, and was never heard of fince.

N O T E.

* *Venus's heart* and *Venus's ear* are the names of two very beautiful fhells.

" To

" To them, Menalcas faid, thy numbers pour ;
" Infult our flocks and blifsful vales no more."
He fpoke ; the heralds knew their fovereign's will,
And hurl'd the fifher down the floping hill :
Headlong he plung'd beneath the liquid plain,
(But not a nymph receiv'd the falling fwain) ;
Then, dropping, rofe ; and, like the rufhing wind,
Impetuous fled, nor caft a look behind :
* He fought the poplar'd banks of winding Po,
But fhunn'd the meads where Ladon's waters flow.

  † Ere through nine radiant figns the flaming fun
His courfe refplendent in the Zodiack run,
The royal damfels, bafhful now no more,
Two lovely boys on one glad morning bore;

I M I T A T I O N S.

  † Amyntas and Amaryllis lived a long and happy life, and
governed the vales of Arcadia. Their generation was very
long-lived, there having been but four defcents in above two
thoufand years, His heir was called Theocritus, who left his
dominions to Virgil, Virgil left his to his fon Spenfer, and
Spenfer was fucceeded by his eldeft-born Philips.

N   O   T   E.

  * This alludes to the Latin compofitions of Sannazarius ; which
have great merit in their kind,

From

From blooming Daphne fair Alexis fprung,
And Colinet on Hyla's bofom hung;
Both o'er the vales of fweet Arcadia reign'd,
And both the manners of their fires retain'd :
* Alexis, fairer than a morn of May,
In glades and forefts tun'd his rural lay,
More foft than rills that through the valley flow,
Or vernal gales that o'er the violets blow ;
He fung the tender woes of artlefs fwains,
Their tuneful contefts, and their amorous pains;
When early fpring has wak'd the breathing flowers,
Or winter hangs with froft the filvery bowers :
† But Colinet in ruder numbers tells
The loves of rufticks, and fair-boding fpells ;
Sings how they fimply pafs the livelong day,
And foftly mourn, or innocently play.

Since them no fhepherd rules th' Arcadian mead,
But filent hangs Menalcas' fatal reed.

N O T E S.

* See Pope's paftorals.
† See the Shepherd's Week, of Gay.

C A I S S A.

C A I S S A.

O R,

THE GAME AT CHESS.

A   P O E M.

Written in the year 1763.

ADVERTISEMENT.

THE firſt idea of the following piece was taken from a Latin poem of Vida, entitled SCACCHIA LUDUS, which was tranſlated into Italian by Marino, and inſerted in the fifteenth Canto of his Adonis: the author thought it fair to make an acknowledgment in the notes for the paſſages which he borrowed from thoſe two poets; but he muſt alſo do them the juſtice to declare, that moſt of the deſcriptions, and the whole ſtory of Caïſſa, which is written in imitation of Ovid, are his own, and their faults muſt be imputed to him only. The characters in the poem are no leſs imaginary than thoſe in the epiſode; in which the invention of Cheſs is poetically aſcribed to Mars, though it is certain that the game was originally brought from India.

✳※✳※✳※✳※✳※✳※✳※✳※✳※

C A I S S A.

*O F armies on the chequer'd field array'd,
And guiltlefs war in pleafing form difplay'd;
When two bold kings contend with vain alarms,
In ivory this, and that in ebon arms;
Sing, fportive maids, that haunt the facred hill
Of Pindus, and the fam'd Pierian rill.
† Thou, joy of all below, and all above,
Mild Venus, queen of laughter, queen of love;

I M I T A T I O N S.

* Ludimus effigiem belli, fimulataque veris
Prælia, buxo acies fictas, et ludicra regna:
Ut gemini inter fe reges, albufque nigerque,
Pro laude oppofiti certent bicoloribus armis.
Dicite, Seriades Nymphæ, certamina tanta.   *Vida.*
† Æneadum genitrix, hominum divûmque voluptas,
Alma Venus! &c.   *Lucretius.*

Leave

Leave thy bright iſland, where on many a roſe
And many a pink thy blooming train repoſe :
Aſſiſt me, goddeſs ! ſince a lovely pair
Command my ſong, like thee divinely fair.

    Near yon cool ſtream, whoſe living waters play,
And riſe tranſlucent in the ſolar ray ;
Beneath the covert of a fragrant bower,
Where ſpring's ſoft influence purpled every flower ;
Two ſmiling nymphs reclin'd in calm retreat,
And envying bloſſoms crouded round their ſeat ;
Here Delia was enthron'd, and by her ſide
The ſweet Sirena, both in beauty's pride :
Thus ſhine two roſes, freſh with early bloom,
That from their native ſtalk diſpenſe perfume ;
Their leaves unfolding to the dawning day
Gems of the glowing mead, and eyes of May.
A band of youths and damſels ſat around,
Their flowing locks with braided myrtle bound ;
Agatis, in the graceful dance admir'd,
And gentle Thyrſis, by the muſe inſpir'd ;
With Sylvia, faireſt of the mirthful train ;
And Daphnis, doom'd to love, yet love in vain.

Now,

Now, whilft a purer blufh o'erfpreads her cheeks,
With foothing accents thus Sirena fpeaks:

" The meads and lawns are ting'd with beamy light,
" And wakeful larks begin their vocal flight;
" Whilft on each bank the dewdrops fweetly fmile;
" What fport, my Delia, fhall the hours beguile?
" Shall heavenly notes, prolong'd with various art,
" Charm the fond ear, and warm the rapturous heart?
" At diftance fhall we view the fylvan chace?
" Or catch with filken lines the finny race?"

Then Delia thus: " Or rather, fince we meet
" By chance affembled in this cool retreat,
" In artful conteft let our warlike train
" Move well-directed o'er the colour'd plain;
" Daphnis, who taught us firft, the play fhall guide;
" Explain its laws, and o'er the field prefide:
" No prize we need, our ardour to inflame;
" We fight with pleafure, if we fight for fame."

The nymph confents: the maids and youths prepare
To view the combat, and the fport to fhare;

But

But Daphnis moſt approv'd the bold deſign,
Whom Love inſtructed, and the tuneful Nine.
. He roſe, and on the cedar table plac'd
A poliſh'd board, with differing colours grac'd;
* Squares eight times eight in equal order lie;
Theſe bright as ſnow, thoſe dark with ſable dye;
Like the broad target by the tortoiſe born,
Or like the hide by ſpotted panthers worn.
Then from a cheſt, with harmleſs heroes ſtor'd,
O'er the ſmooth plain two well-wrought hoſts he pour'd;
The champions burn'd their rivals to aſſail,
† Twice eight in black, twice eight in milkwhite mail;

I M I T A T I O N S.

* Sexaginta inſunt et quatuor ordine ſedes
  Octono; parte ex omni, via limite quadrat
  Ordinibus paribus; necnon forma omnibus una
  Sedibus, æquale et ſpatium, ſed non color unus:
  Alternant ſemper variæ, ſubeuntque viciſſim
  Albentes nigris; teſtudo picta ſuperne
  Qualia devexo geſtat diſcrimina tergo.
                                        Vida.

† Agmina bina pari numeroque, et viribus æquis,
  Bis niveâ cum veſte octo, totidemque nigranti.
  Ut variæ facies, pariter ſunt et ſua cuique
  Nomina, diverſum munus, non æqua poteſtas.
                                        Vida.

In

In fhape and ftation different, as in name,
Their motions various, nor their power the fame.
Say, mufe! (for Jove has nought from thee conceal'd)
Who form'd the legions on the level field ?

High in the midft the reverend kings appear,
And o'er the reft their pearly fcepters rear :
One folemn ftep, majeftically flow,
They gravely move, and fhun the dangerous foe ;
If e'er they call, the watchful fubjects fpring,
And die with rapture if they fave their king ;
On him the glory of the day depends,
He once imprifon'd, all the conflict ends.

The queens exulting near their conforts ftand ;
Each bears a deadly falchion in her hand ;
Now here, now there, they bound with furious pride,
And thin the trembling ranks from fide to fide ;
Swift as Camilla flying o'er the main,
Or lightly fkimming o'er the dewy plain :
Fierce as they feem, fome bold Plebeian fpear
May pierce their fhield, or ftop their full career.

The valiant guards, their minds on havock bent,
Fill the next fquares, and watch the royal tent ;

K   Though

Though weak their fpears, though dwarfifh be their height,
* Compact they move, the bulwark of the fight.

To right and left the martial wings difplay
Their fhining arms, and ftand in clofe array.
Behold, four archers, eager to advance,
Send the light reed, and rufh with fidelong glance;
Through angles ever they affault the foes,
True to the colour, which at firft they chofe.
Then four bold knights for courage fam'd and fpeed,
Each knight exalted on a prancing fteed:
† Their arching courfe no vulgar limit knows,
Tranfverfe they leap, and aim infidious blows:

IMITATIONS.

† Il cavallo leggier per dritta lifta,
  Come gli altri, l'arringo unqua non fende,
  Mà la lizza attraverfa, e fiero in vifta
  Curvo in giro, e lunato il falto ftende,
  E fempre nel faltar due cafe acquifta,
  Quel colore abbandona, e quefto prende.
               Marino, Adone. 15.

N O T E.

* The chief art in the Tacticks of Chefs confifts in the nice con-
duct of the royal pawns; in fupporting them againft every attack;
and, if they are taken, in fupplying their places with others equally
fupported: a principle, on which the fuccefs of the game in great
meafure depends, though it feems to be omitted by the very accu-
rate Vida.
                                Nor

Nor friends, nor foes, their rapid force reſtrain,
By one quick bound two changing ſquares they gain;
From varying hues renew the fierce attack,
And ruſh from black to white, from white to black.
Four ſolemn elephants the ſides defend;
Beneath the load of ponderous towers they bend:
In one unalter'd line they tempt the fight;
Now cruſh the left, and now o'erwhelm the right.
Bright in the front the dauntleſs ſoldiers raiſe
Their poliſh'd ſpears; their ſteely helmets blaze:
Prepar'd they ſtand the daring foe to ſtrike,
Direct their progreſs, but their wounds oblique.

Now ſwell th' embattled troops with hoſtile rage,
And clang their ſhields, impatient to engage;
When Daphnis thus: A varied plain behold,
Where fairy kings their mimick tents unfold,
As Oberon, and Mab, his wayward queen,
Lead forth their armies on the daiſied green.
No mortal hand the wondrous ſport contriv'd,
By Gods invented, and from Gods deriv'd;

K 2   From

* From them the Britifh nymphs receiv'd the game,
And play each morn beneath the cryftal Thame;
Hear then the tale, which they to Colin fung,
As idling o'er the lucid wave he hung.

A lovely Dryad rang'd the Thracian wild,
Her air enchanting, and her afpect mild;
To chafe the bounding hart was all her joy,
Averfe from Hymen, and the Cyprian boy;
O'er hills and valleys was her beauty fam'd,
And fair Caiffa was the damfel nam'd.
Mars faw the maid; with deep furprize he gaz'd,
Admir'd her fhape, and every gefture prais'd:
His golden bow the child of Venus bent,
And through his breaft a piercing arrow fent:
The reed was Hope; the feathers, keen Defire;
The point, her eyes; the barbs, ethereal fire.
Soon to the nymph he pour'd his tender ftrain;
The haughty Dryad fcorn'd his amorous pain:

I M I T A T I O N S.

* Quæ quondam fub aquis gaudent fpectacla tueri
  Nereides, vaftique omnis gens accola ponti;
  Siquando placidum mare, et humida regna quierunt.

Vida.

He

He told his woes, where'er the maid he found,
And ftill he prefs'd, yet ftill Caiffa frown'd;
But ev'n her frowns (ah, what might fmiles have done!)
Fir'd all his foul, and all his fenfes won.
He left his car, by raging tigers drawn,
And lonely wander'd o'er the dufky lawn;
Then lay defponding near a murmuring ftream,
And fair Caïffa was his plaintive theme.
A Naiad heard him from her moffy bed,
And through the cryftal rais'd her placid head;
Then mildly fpake: " O thou, whom love infpires,
" Thy tears will nourifh, not allay thy fires.
" The fmiling bloffoms drink the pearly dew;
" And ripening fruit the feather'd race purfue;
" The fcaly fhoals devour the filken weeds;
" Love on our fighs, and on our forrow feeds.
" Then weep no more; but, ere thou canft obtain
" Balm to thy wounds, and folace to thy pain,
" With gentle art thy martial look beguile;
" Be mild, and teach thy rugged brow to fmile.
" Canft thou no play, no foothing game devife,
" To make thee lovely in the damfel's eyes?
" So may thy prayers affuage the fcornful dame,
" And ev'n Caïffa own a mutual flame."

K 3

" Kin

" Kind nymph, faid Mars, thy counfel I approve;

" Art, only art, her ruthlefs breaft can move.

" But when? or how? Thy dark difcourfe explain:

" So may thy ftream ne'er fwell with gufhing rain;

" So may thy waves in one pure current flow,

" And flowers eternal on thy border blow!"

To whom the maid replied with fmiling mien:

" Above the palace of the Paphian queen

" * Love's brother dwells, a boy of graceful port,

" By gods nam'd Euphron, and by mortals Sport:

" Seek him; to faithful ears unfold thy grief,

" And hope, ere morn return, a fweet relief.

" His temple hangs below the azure fkies;

" Seeft thou yon argent cloud? 'Tis there it lies."

This faid, fhe funk beneath the liquid plain,

And fought the manfion of her blue-hair'd train.

IMITATIONS.

* Ecco d' aftuto ingegno, e pronta mano
  Garzon, che fempre fcherza, e vola ratto,
  Gioco s'apella, ed è *d'* amor germano.

Marino, Adone. 15.

Meantime

Meantime the god, elate with heart-felt joy,
Had reach'd the temple of the fportful boy;
He told Caïffa's charms, his kindled fire,
The Naiad's counfel, and his warm defire.
" Be fwift, he added, give my paffion aid;
" A god requefts."—He fpake, and Sport obey'd.
He fram'd a tablet of celeftial mold,
Inlay'd with fquares of filver and of gold;
Then of two metals form'd the warlike band,
That here compact in fhow of battle ftand;
He taught the rules that guide the penfive game,
And call'd it *Caïffa* from the Dryad's name:
(Whence Albion's fons, who moft its praife confefs,
Approv'd the play, and nam'd it thoughtful *Chefs.*)
The god delighted thank'd indulgent Sport;
Then grafp'd the board, and left his airy court.
With radiant feet he pierc'd the clouds; nor ftay'd,
Till in the woods he faw the beauteous maid:
Tir'd with the chafe the damfel fat reclin'd,
Her girdle loofe, her bofom unconfin'd.
He took the figure of a wanton Faun,
And ftood before her on the flowery lawn;
Then fhow'd his tablet: pleas'd the nymph furvey'd
The lifelefs troops in glittering ranks difplay'd;

She

She afk'd the wily fylvan to explain
The various motions of the fplendid train;
With eager heart fhe caught the winning lore,
And thought ev'n Mars lefs hateful than before :
" What fpell, faid fhe, deceiv'd my carelefs mind?
" The god was fair, and I was moft unkind."
She fpoke, and faw the changing Faun affume
A milder afpect, and a fairer bloom ;
His wreathing horns, that from his temples grew,
Flow'd down in curls of bright celeftial hue;
The dappled hairs, that veil'd his lovelefs face,
Blaz'd into beams, and fhow'd a heavenly grace;
The fhaggy hide, that mantled o'er his breaft,
Was foften'd to a fmooth tranfparent veft,
That through its folds his vigorous bofom fhow'd,
And nervous limbs, where youthful ardour glow'd ;
(Had Venus view'd him in thofe blooming charms,
Not Vulcan's net had forc'd her from his arms.)
With goatlike feet no more he mark'd the ground,
But braided flowers his filken fandals bound. .
The Dryad blufh'd; and, as he prefs'd her, fmil'd,
Whilft all his cares one tender glance beguil'd,

He

He ends: *To arms,* the maids and ftriplings cry;
To arms, the groves and founding vales reply.
Sirena led to war the fwarthy crew,
And Delia thofe that bore the lily's hue.
Who firft, O mufe, began the bold attack;
The white refulgent, or the mournful black?
Fair Delia firft, as favouring lots ordain,
Moves her pale legions tow'rd the fable train:
From thought to thought her lively fancy flies,
Whilft o'er the board fhe darts her fparkling eyes.

    At length the warriour moves with haughty ftrides;
Who from the plain the fnowy king divides:
With equal hafte his fwarthy rival bounds;
His quiver rattles, and his buckler founds:
Ah! haplefs youths, with fatal warmth you burn;
Laws, ever fix'd, forbid you to return.
Then from the wing a fhort-liv'd fpearman flies,
Unfafely bold, and fee! he dies, he dies:
The dark-brow'd hero, with one vengeful blow
Of life and place deprives his ivory foe.
Now rufh both armies o'er the burnifh'd field,
Hurl the fwift dart, and rend the burfting fhield.

                                Here

Here furious knights on fiery courfers prance,
Here archers fpring, and lofty towers advance.
But fee! the white-rob'd Amazon beholds
Where the dark hoft its opening van unfolds:
Soon as her eye difcerns the hoftile maid,
By ebon fhield, and ebon helm betray'd;
Seven fquares fhe paffes with majeftick mien,
And ftands triumphant o'er the falling queen.
Perplex'd, and forrowing at his confort's fate,
The monarch burn'd with rage, defpair, and hate:
Swift from his zone th' avenging blade he drew,
And, mad with ire, the proud virago flew,
Meanwhile fweet-fmiling Delia's wary king
Retir'd from fight behind his circling wing.

Long time the war in equal balance hung;
Till, unforefeen, an ivory courfer fprung,
And, wildly prancing in an evil hour,
Attack'd at once the monarch and the tower:
Sirena blufh'd; for, as the rules requir'd,
Her injur'd fovereign to his tent retir'd;
Whilft her loft caftle leaves his threatening height,
And adds new glory to th' exulting knight.

At

At this, pale fear opprefs'd the drooping maid,
And on her cheek the rofe began to fade:
A cryftal tear, that ftood prepar'd to fall,
She wip'd in filence, and conceal'd from all;
From all but Daphnis: He remark'd her pain,
And faw the weaknefs of her ebon train;
Then gently fpoke; " Let me your lofs fupply,
" And either nobly win, or nobly die;
" Me oft has fortune crown'd with fair fuccefs,
" And led to triumph in the fields of Chefs."
He faid: the willing nymph her place refign'd,
And fat at diftance on the bank reclin'd.
Thus when Minerva call'd her chief to arms,
And Troy's high turret fhook with dire alarms,
The Cyprian goddefs wounded left the plain,
And Mars engag'd a mightier force in vain,

Straight Daphnis leads his fquadron to the field;
(To Delia's arms 'tis ev'n a joy to yield.)
Each guileful fnare, and fubtle art he tries,
But finds his art lefs powerful than her eyes:
Wifdom and ftrength fuperiour charms obey;
And beauty, beauty, wins the long-fought day.

By

By this a hoary chief, on flaughter bent,
Approach'd the gloomy king's unguarded tent ;
Where, late, his confort fpread difmay around,
Now her dark corfe lies bleeding on the ground.
Hail, happy youth! thy glories not unfung
Shall live eternal on the poet's tongue ;
For thou fhalt foon receive a fplendid change,
And o'er the plain with nobler fury range.
The fwarthy leaders faw the ftorm impend,
And ftrove in vain their fovereign to defend :
Th' invader wav'd his filver lancè in air,
And flew like lightning to the fatal fquare;
His limbs dilated in a moment grew
To ftately height, and widen'd to the view ;
More fierce his look, more lion-like his mien,
Sublime he mov'd, and feem'd a warriour queen.
As when the fage on fome unfolding plant
Has caught a wandering fly, or frugal ant,
His hand the microfcopick frame applies,
And lo! a bright-hair'd monfter meets his eyes;
He fees new plumes in flender cafes roll'd ;
Here ftain'd with azure, there bedropp'd with gold ;
Thus, on the alter'd chief both armies gaze,
And both the kings are fix'd with deep amaze.

The

The fword, which arm'd the fnow-white maid before,
He now affumes, and hurls the fpear no more;
Then fprings indignant on the dark-rob'd band,
And knights and archers feel his deadly hand,
Now flies the monarch of the fable fhield,
His legions vanquifh'd, o'er the lonely field :
* So when the morn, by rofy courfers drawn,
With pearls and rubies fows the verdant lawn,
Whilft each pale ftar from heaven's blue vault retires,
Still Venus gleams, and laft of all expires.
He hears, where'er he moves, the dreadful found;
Check the deep vales, and *Check* the woods rebound.
No place remains : he fees the certain fate,
And yields his throne to ruin, and Checkmate.

A brighter blufh o'erfpreads the damfel's cheeks,
And mildly thus the conquer'd ftripling fpeaks :
" A double triumph, Delia, haft thou won,
" By Mars protected, and by Venus' fon;

IMITATIONS.

* ———— Medio rex æquore inermis
Conftitit amiffis fociis; velut æthere in alto
Expulit ardentes flammas ubi lutea bigis
Luciferis Aurora, tuus pulcherrimus ignis
'Lucet adhuc, Venus, et cœlo mox ultimus exit.

Vida, ver. 604.

" The

" The firſt with conqueſt crowns thy matchleſs art,
" The ſecond points thoſe eyes at Daphnis' heart."
She ſmil'd; the nymphs and amorous youths ariſe,
And own, that beauty gain'd the nobler prize.

Low in their cheſt the mimick troops were lay'd,
* And peaceful ſlept the ſable hero's ſhade.

---

* A parody of the laſt line in Pope's tranſlation of the Iliad,
" And peaceful ſlept the mighty Hector's ſhade :"

C A R.

CARMINUM LIBER.

I. ODE SINICA.

Vides ut agros dulce gemmatos lavet
    Argenteus rivi latex ;
Virides ut aura ftridulo modulamine
    Arundines interftrepat :
Sic, fic, amœno cincte virtutum choro
    Princeps, amabiliter nites.
Ut maximo labore, & arte maximâ
    Effingit artifex ebur,
Sic ad benignitatem amica civium
    Blandè figuras pectora.
Ut delicata gemmulam expolit manus
    Fulgore lucentem aureo,

Sic

Sic civitatem mitium gaudes tuam
  Ornare morum lumine.
O quàm verenda micat in oculis lenitas !
  Minantur & rident fimul.
O quanta pulchro dignitas vultu patet,
  Et quantus inceffu decor ! ·
Scilicet, amœno cinĉte virtutum choro
  Priaceps, amabiliter nites.
Annon per omne, veris inftar, feculum
  Memoria florefcet tui ?

II. ODE PERSICA.

JAM rofa purpureum caput explicat. Adfit, amici,
  Suavis voluptatum cohors :
    Sic monuêre fenes.
Nunc læti fumus ; at citius læta avolat ætas,
    Quin facra mutemus mero
      Stragula nectareo ?

· Dulce

Dulcè gemit zephyrus : ridentem mitte puellam,
  Quam molli in amplexu tenens
    Pocula læta bibam.
Tange chelyn. Sævit fortuna; at mitte querelas :
  Cur non canoros barbiti
    Elicimus modulos ?
En! florum regina nitet rofa. Fundite vini,
  Quod amoris extinguat facem,
    Nectareos latices..
Suavè loquens Philomela vocor : quî fiat ut umbrâ
  Tectus rofarum nexili
    (Veris avis) taceam ?

***

III.   A L T E R A.

AFFER fcyphos, & dulcè ridentis meri
  Purpureos latices
Effunde largiùs, puer.
Nam vinum amores lenit adolefcentium,
  Difficilefque fenum
  Emollit ægritudines.

Solem

Solem merum æmulatur, & lunam calix;
  Nectareis foveat
Dic luna solem amplexibus.

Flammas nitentes sparge: vini scilicet
  Fervidioris aquam
Flammæ nitentis æmulam.

Quòd si rosarum fragilis avolat decor,
  Sparge, puer, liquidas·
·Vini rubescentis rosas.

Si devium Philomela deserit nemus,
  Pocula læta canant
Non elaboratum melos.

Injuriofæ sperne fortunæ minas;
  Lætaque mœstitiam
Depellat informem chelys.

Somnus beatos, somnus amplexûs dabit:
  Da mihi dulce merum
Somnum quod alliciat levem.

Dulce est madere vino. Da calices novos,
  Ut placidâ madidus
Oblivione perfruar.

Scyphum affer alterum, puer, deinde alterum:
  Seu vetitum fuerit,
Amice, seu licitum, bibam.

IV. OD

$\times\times\times\times\times\times\times\times\times\times\times\times\times\times\times\times\times\times\times$

IV. ODE ARABICA.

AD FABULLUM.

DULCI triſtitiam vino lavere, aut, nitente lunâ,
  Multâ reclines in rosâ
Urgere blandis oſculis puellas;
Aut, dum prata levi pulſat pede delicata virgo
  Comam renodans auream,
  Molli cupidinis tepere flammâ:
Aut, dum blanda aures recreat lyra, floreo ſub antro
  Ad ſuave zephyrorum melos
  Rore advocati ſpargier ſoporis:
Hæc ver purpureum dat gaudia, comis & juventas,
  His, mite dum tempus favet,
  Decet vacare, dumque ridet annus.
Quicunque aut rerum domini ſumus, aut graves coacti
  Curas egeſtatis pati,
  Debemur aſperæ, Fabulle, morti.

✳✳✳✳✳✳✳✳✳✳✳✳✳✳✳✳✳✳✳✳✳✳✳✳

V.   AD LÆLIUM.

VESTIMENTA tuis grata fororibus,
   Et donem lapides, quos vel alit Tagi
 Fluctus, vel celer undâ
      Ganges auriferâ lavit,
Læli, fi mea fit dives opum domus :
Quid mittam addubito.   Scilicet haud mea
   Servo carmina blandis
      Nympharum auribus infolens,
Quarum tu potior pectora candidis
Mulces alloquiis, te potiorem amat
   Mufa, utcunque puellæ
      Pulfas Æoliæ fides.
Quin illis acies mittere commodus
Tornatas meditor, quæ bicoloribus
   Armis confpiciendæ
      Bella innoxia deftinant ;

Qualis

Qualis propter aquas aut Lacedæmoni
Eurotæ gelidas, aut Tiberis vada,
   Cornicum manus albis
     Nigrans certat oloribus.
Cur non fub viridi ludimus ilicis
Umbrâ fuppofiti ? Dic veniat genis
   Ridens Lydia pulchris,
     Et faltare decens Chloe :
Dic reddant mihi me.   Ludite, virgines;
Me teftudineis aut Venerem modis
   Dicente, aut juvenilis
     Telum dulce Cupidinis.

❋❋❋❋❋❋❋❋❋❋❋❋❋❋❋❋❋❋❋❋

VI. A D   L U N A M:

CŒLI dulcè nitens decus,
   Lentâ lora manu, Cynthia, corripe :
Pulchræ teƈta peto Chloës,
Et labrum rofeo neƈtare fuavius.

L 3

Non

Non prædator ut improbus,
Per fylvas propero, te duce, devias ;
  Nec, dum lux radiat tua,
Ultricem meditor figere cufpidem,

  Quem tu, mitis Amor, femel
Placatum tepidâ lenieris face,
  Illum deferuit furor,
Et telum facili decidit è manu.

  Nec delicta per & nefas
Furtiva immeritus gaudia perfequor ;
  Blandâ victa Chloë prece
Peplum rejiciet purpureum libens,

VII. A D   V E N E R E M,

O R O te teneri blanda Cupidinis
  Mater, cœruleis edita fluctibus,
Quæ grati fruticeta accolis Idali,
Herbofamque Amathunta, & viridem Cnidon,
Oro, Pyrrha, meis cedat amoribus,
Quæ nunc, Tænariâ immitior æfculo,

                Mœ rentis

Mœrentis Licinî follicitum melos
Ridet. Non liquidæ carmine tibiæ,
Non illam Æoliis illacrymabilem
Plectris dimoveat, lenis ut arduam
Cervicem tepidum flectat ad ofculum.
(Quantum eft & vacuis nectar in ofculis!)
Quod fi carminibus mitior applicet
Aures illa meis, fi (rigidum gelu
Te folvente) pari me tepeat face,
Te propter liquidum fonticuli vitrum,
Ponam confpicuo marmore lucidam,
Te cantans Paphiam, teque Amathufiam
Pellam gramineum ter pede cefpitem,
Tum nigranti hederâ & tempora laureâ
Cingam, tunc hilares eliciam modos :
At nunc me juvenum prætereuntium
Me ridet comitum cœtus amabilis ;
Et ludens puerorum in plateis cohors
Oftendit digitis me, quia langueo
Demiffis oculis, me, quia fomnia
Abrupta haud facili virgine faucium
Monftrant, & violâ pallidior gena.

✻✻✻✻✻✻✻✻✻✻✻✻✻✻✻✻✻✻✻✻✻✻✻✻

VIII. AD EANDEM.

P ERFIDO ridens Erycina vultu,
  Seu Joci mater, tenerique Amoris,
Seu Paphi regina potens, Cyprique
        Laetior audis,

Linque jucundam Cnidon, & corufcum
Dirigens currum levis huc vocanti,
Huc veni, & tecum properet foluto
        Crine Thalia.

Jam venis! nubes placidi ferenas
Pafferes findunt; fuper albicantes
Dum volant fylvas, celerefque verfant
        Leniter alas.

Rurfus ad cœlum fugiunt. Sed almâ
Dulcè fubridens facie, loquelam
Melle conditam liquido jacentis
        Fundis in aurem,

                            " Qua

"Qua tepes, inquis, Licini, puellâ,
" Lucidis venanti oculis amantes ?
" Cur doces mœstas refonare lucum,
    " Care, querelas ?
" Dona fi ridet tua, dona mittet ;
" Sive te molli rofeos per hortos
" Hinnulo vitat levior, fequetur
    " Ipfa fugacem."
Per tuos oro, dea mitis, ignes,
Pectus ingratæ rigidum Corinnæ
Lenias. Et te, Venus alma, amore
    Forfit Adonis.

EX FERDUSII POETÆ PERSICI
POEMATE HEROICO.

SAMUS, ut aurato cinctum diademate regem
  Vidit ovans, excelfa ferebat ad atria greffum ;
Quem rex ad meritos facilis provexit honores,
Et fecum in folio juffit confidere eburneo,

                             Cælato

Cælato rutilanti auro, infertifque pyropis.

Magnanimum affatus tum blandâ heroä loquelâ,

Multa fuper fociis, fuper armis multa rogabat,

Jam, quantos aleret tellus Hyrcana gigantas,

Jam, quâ parta manu nova fit victoria Perfis:

Cui dux hæc memori parens eft voce locutus.

Venimus ad caftra hoftilis, rex maxime, gentis;

Gens eft dura, ferox; non afpera fævior errat

Per dumeta leo, non fylvâ tigris in atrâ;

Non equus in lætis Arabum it velocior agris.

Cùm fubito trepidam pervenit rumor in urbem

Adventare aciem, queruli per tecta, per arces,

Auditi gemitûs, & non lætabile murmur:

Ilicet æratâ fulgentes caffide turmas

Eduxere viri; pars vaftos fufa per agros,

Pars monte in rigido, aut depreffa valle fedebat:

Horruit ære acies, tantæque a pulvere nubes

Exortæ, ut pulchrum tegeret jubar ætherius fol.

Quale in arenofo nigrarum colle laborat

Formicarum agmen, congeftaque farra reponit;

Aut qualis culicum leviter ftridentibus alis

Turba volans, tenues ciet importuna fufurros;

Tales profiluere. Nepos ante agmina Salmi

Cercius emicuit, quo non fuit ardua pinus

Altior,

Altior, aut vernans excelſo in monte cupreſſus.
At Perſarum artûs gelida formidine ſolvi
Arguit & tremor, & laxato in corpore pallor :
Hoc vidi, & valido torquens haſtiie lacerto
Per medias juſſi, duce me, penetrare phalangas ;
Irruit alatus ſonipes, ceu torvus in arvis
Æthiopum latis elephas, neque ſenſit habenam :
Militibus vires rediêre, & priſtina virtus.
Ac velut, undantis cùm ſurgant flumina Nili,
Et refluant, avidis haud injucunda colonis,
Pinguia frugiferis implentur fluctibus arva ;
Sic terra innumeris agitata eſt illa catervis :
Cum ſtrepitum audierit noſtrum, ingentemque fragorem
Findentis galeas & ferrea ſcuta bipennis,
Cercius, horrifico complens loca vaſta boatu,
In me flexit equum, me crudeli enſe petebat,
Captivumque arcto voluit conſtringere nodo :
Fruſtra ; nam, lunans habilem nec ſegniter arcum,
Populeas miſi duro mucrone ſagittas,
Flammarum ritu, aut per nubila fulminis acti :
Ille tamen celeri ruit impete, noſque morantes
Increpitat, letum minitans, rigidaſve catenas :
Ut verò acceſſit violenti turbinis inſtar,
Pulſus ut & clypeus clypeo eſt, & caſſide caſſis

Illum

Illum infurgentem, dirumque infligere vulnus
Conantem, arripui, qua difcolor ilia cinxit
Balteus, & rutilis fubnexa eft fibula baccis.
Strenua tum valido molimine brachia verfans
E ftratis evulfi equitem, qui pronus, inermis,
Decidit, & rabido frendens campum ore momordit;
Pectora cui nivea, & ferratâ cufpide coftas
Transfodi, madidam defluxit fanguis in herbam
Purpureus, triftifque elapfa eft vita fub umbras.
Haud mora, diffugiunt hoftes, ductore perempto,
Saxa per & colles; noftris victoria turmis
Affulfit, cæfofque doles, Hyrcania, natos.
Sic pereant, quicunque tuo, rex optime, fceptro,
Qui premis imperio ftellas, parere recufent!
Dixit; & heroas Perfarum rector ovantes
Laudibus in cœlum tollit; jubet inde beatas
Inftaurari epulas, & pocula dulcia poni:
Conventum eft, textoque fuper difcumbitur auro.

ELEGIA

ELEGIA ARABICA.

FULGUR an è densâ vibratum nube corufcat?
    An rofeas nudat Leila pudica genas?
Bacciferumne celer fruticetum devorat ignis?
    Siderea an Solimæ lumina dulcè micant?
Nardus an Hageri, an fpirant violaria Meccæ,
    Candida odoriferis an venit Azza comis?
Quàm juvat ah! patrios memori tenuiffe receffûs
    Mente, per ignotos dum vagor exul agros?
Valle fub umbrofâ, pallens ubi luget amator,
    Num colit affuetos mollis amica lares?
Jamne cient raucum præfracta tonitrua murmur
    Montibus, effufæ quos rigat imber aquæ?
An tua, dum fundit primum lux alma ruborem,
    Lympha, Azibe, meam pellet, ut ante, fitim?
Quot mea felices vidiftis gaudia, campi,
    Gaudia væ! mifero non renovanda mihi?
Ecquis apud Nagedi lucos aut pafcua Tudæ
    Paftor amatorum fpefque metufque canit?

                                Ecquis

Ecquis ait, gelidâ Salæ dum valle recumbit,

    " Heu ! quid Cademeo in monte fodalis agit ?"

Num graciles rident hyemalia frigora myrti ?

    Num viret in folitis lotos amata locis ?

Num vernant humiles in aprico colle myricæ ?

    Ne malus has oculus, ne mala lædat hyems !

An mea Alegiades, dulciſſima turba, puellæ

    Curant, an Zephyris irrita vota dabunt ?

An viridem faliunt, nullo venante, per hortum

    Hinnuleique citi, capreolique leves ?

Vifamne umbriferos, loca dilectiſſima, faltus,

    Ducit ubi facilem læta Noama chorum ?

Num Daregi ripas patulâ tegit arbutus umbrâ,

    Ah ! quoties lacrymis humida facta meis ?

Grata quis antra colit, nobis abfentibus, Amri,

    Antra puellarum quàm bene nota gregi ?

Forfan amatores Meccanâ in valle reductos

    Abfentis Solimæ commeminiſſe juvat.

Tempus erit, levibus quo pervigilata cachinnis

    Nox dabit unanimi gaudia plena choro;

Quo dulces juvenum fpirabit cœtus amores,

    Et lætos avidâ combibet aure modos.

FABULA

FABULA PERSICA.

R IGANTE molles imbre campos Perfidis,
    E nube in æquor lapfa pluviæ guttula eft ;
Quæ, cùm reluctans eloqui fineret pudor,
" Quid hoc loci ? inquit, quid rei mifella fum ?
" Quò me repente, ah ! quò redactam fentio ?"
Cùm fe verecundanti animulâ fperneret,
Illam recepit gemmeo concha in finu ;
Tandemque tenuis aquula facta eft unio ;
Nunc in coronâ læta Regis emicat,
Sibi non placere quanta fit virtus, docens.

AD

❀❋❀❋❀❋❀❋❀❋❀❋❀❋❀❋❀❋❀❋❀❋❀❋❀

AD MUSAM.

VALE, Camena, blanda cultrix ingenî,
   Virtutis altrix, mater eloquentiæ !
Linquenda alumno eſt laurus & chelys tuo :
At tu dearum dulcium dulciſſima,
Seu Suada mavis ſive Pitho dicier,
A te receptus in tuâ vivam fide :
Mihi ſit, oro, non inutilis toga,
Nec indiſerta lingua, nec turpis manus

ESSAYS.

E S S A Y S.

E S S A Y I.

On the Poetry of the Eaſtern Nations.

A R A B I A, I mean that part of it, which we call the *Happy,* and which the *Aſiaticks* know by the name of *Yemen,* feems to be the only country in the world, in which we can properly lay the ſcene of paſtoral poetry ; becauſe no nation at this day can vie with the *Arabians* in the delightfulneſs of their climate, and the ſimplicity of their manners. There is a valley, indeed, to the north of *Indoſtan,* called *Caſhmere,* which, according to an account written by a native of it, is a perfect garden, exceedingly fruitful, and watered by a thouſand rivulets : but when its inhabitants were ſubdued by the ſtratagem of a *Mogul* prince, they loſt their happineſs with their liberty, and *Arabia* retained its old title without any rival to diſpute it. Theſe are not the

fancies

fancies of a poet : the beauties of *Yemen* are proved by the concurrent teſtimony of all travellers, by the deſcriptions of them in all the writings of *Aſia*, and by the nature and ſituation of the country itſelf, which lies between the eleventh and fifteenth degrees of northern latitude, under a ſerene ſky, and expoſed to the moſt favourable influence of the ſun; it is encloſed on one ſide by vaſt rocks and deſerts, and defended on the other by a tempeſtuous ſea, ſo that it ſeems to have been deſigned by providence for the moſt ſecure, as well as the moſt beautiful, region of the Eaſt. I am at a loſs to conceive, what induced the illuſtrious Prince *Cantemir* to contend that *Yemen* is properly a part of *India* ; for, not to mention *Ptolemy*, and the other ancients, who conſidered it as a province of *Arabia*, nor to inſiſt on the language of the country, which is pure *Arabick*, it is deſcribed by the *Aſiaticks* themſelves as a large diviſion of that peninſula, which they call *Jezeiratul Arab* ; and there is no more colour for annexing it to *India*, becauſe the ſea, which waſhes one ſide of it, is looked upon by ſome writers as belonging to the great *Indian* ocean, than there would be for annexing it to *Perſia*, becauſe it is bounded on another ſide by the *Perſian* gulf. Its principal cities are *Sanaa*, uſually conſidered as its metropolis; *Zebid*, a commercial town, that lies in a large plain near the ſea of *Omman*; and *Aden*, ſurrounded with pleaſant gardens and woods, which is ſituated eleven degrees from the *Equator*, and ſeventy-ſix from the *Fortunate Iſlands*, or *Canaries*, where the geographers of *Aſia* fix their firſt meridian.

meridian. It is obfervable that *Aden*, in the Eaftern dialects, is precifely the fame word with *Eden*, which we apply to the garden of paradife : it has two fenfes, according to a flight difference in its pronunciation; its firft meaning is *a fettled abode*, its fecond, *delight, foftnefs*, or *tranquillity :* the word *Eden* had, probably, one of thefe fenfes in the facred text, though we ufe it as a proper name. We may alfo obferve in this place that *Yemen* itfelf takes its name from a word, which fignifies *verdure*, and *felicity*; for in thofe fultry climates, the frefhnefs of the fhade, and the coolnefs of water, are ideas almoft infeparable from that of happinefs ; and this may be a reafon why moft of the *Oriental* nations agree in a tradition concerning a delightful fpot, where the firft inhabitants of the earth were placed before their fall. The ancients, who gave the name of *Eudaimon*, or *Happy*, to this country, either meaned to tranflate the word *Yemen*, or, more probably, only alluded to the valuable fpice-trees, and balfamick plants, that grow in it, and, without fpeaking poetically, give a real perfume to the air : the writer of an old hiftory of the *Turkifh* empire fays, " *The air of Egypt fometimes in fummer is like* " *any fweet perfume, and almoft fuffocates the fpirits, caufed* " *by the wind that brings the odours of the Arabian fpices :*" now it is certain that all poetry receives a very confiderable ornament from the beauty of natural images ; as the rofes of *Sharon*, the verdure of *Carmel*, the vines of *Engaddi*, and the dew of *Hermon*, are the fources of many pleafing metaphors and comparifons in the facred

poet

poetry : thus the odours of *Yemen,* the musk of *Hadra-mut,* and the pearls of *Omman,* supply the *Arabian* poets with a great variety of allusions; and, if the remark of *Hermogenes* be just, that whatever is *delightful to the senses* produces the *Beautiful* when it is described, where can we find so much beauty as in the *Eastern* poems, which turn chiefly upon the loveliest objects in nature ?

To pursue this topick yet farther : it is an observation of *Demetrius Phalereus,* in his elegant treatise upon style, that it is not easy to write on agreeable subjects in a disagreeable manner, and that beautiful *expressions* naturally rise with beautiful images; *for which reason,* says he, *nothing can be more pleasing than Sappho's poetry, which contains the description of gardens, and banquets, flowers and fruits, fountains and meadows, nightingales and turtle-doves, loves and graces :* thus, when she speaks of *a stream softly murmuring among the branches, and the Zephyrs playing through the leaves, with a sound that brings on a quiet slumber,* her lines flow without labour as smoothly as the rivulet she describes. I may have altered the words of *Demetrius,* as I quote them by memory, but this is the general sense of his remark, which, if it be not rather specious than just, must induce us to think, that the poets of the *East* may vie with those of *Europe* in *the graces of their diction,* as well as in the loveliness of their images : but we must not believe that the *Arabian* poetry can please only by its descriptions of *beauty*; since the gloomy and terrible objects, which produce the *sublime,* when they

are

are aptly defcribed, are no where more common than in the *Defert* and *Stony Arabia's*; and, indeed, we fee nothing fo frequently painted by the poets of thofe countries, as wolves and lions, precipices and forefts, rocks and wildernefles.

If we allow the natural objects, with which the *Arabs* are perpetually converfant, to be *fublime*, and *beautiful*, our next ftep muft be, to confefs that their comparifons, metaphors, and allegories are fo likewife ; for an allegory is only a ftring of metaphors, a metaphor is only a fhort fimile, and the fineft fimiles are drawn from natural objects. It is true that many of the *Eaftern* figures are common to other nations, but fome of them receive a propriety from the manners of the *Arabians*, who dwell in the plains and woods, which would be loft, if they came from the inhabitants of cities: thus *the dew of liberality*, and the *odour of reputation*, are metaphors ufed by moft people; but they are wonderfully proper in the mouths of thofe, who have fo much need of. being refrefhed by *the dews*, and who gratify their fenfe of fmelling with the *fweeteft odours* in the world. Again; it is very ufual in all countries to make frequent allufions to the brightnefs of the celeftial luminaries, which give their light to all ; but the metaphors taken from them have an additional beauty, if we confider them as made by a nation, who pafs moft of their nights in the open air, or in tents, and confequently fee the moon and ftars in their greateft fplendour. This way of confidering

their

their poetical figures will give many of them a grace, which they would not have in our languages : fo, when they compare *the foreheads of their miſtreſſes to the morning, their locks to the night, their faces to the ſun, to the moon, or the bloſſoms of jaſmine, their cheeks to roſes or ripe fruit, their teeth to pearls, hail-ſtones, and ſnow-drops, their eyes to the flowers of the narciſſus, their curled hair to black ſcorpions and to hyacinths, their lips to rubies or wine, the form of their breaſts to pomegranates, and the colour of them to ſnow, their ſhape to that of a pine-tree, and their ſtature to that of a cypreſs, a palm-tree, or a javelin, &c.* theſe comparifons, many of which would feem forced in our idioms, have undoubtedly a great delicacy in theirs, and affect their minds in a peculiar manner ; yet upon the whole their fimiles are very juſt and ſtriking, as that of *the blue eyes of a fine woman, bathed in tears, to violets dropping with dew,* and that of *a warriour, advancing at the head of his army, to an eagle ſailing through the air, and piercing the clouds with his wings.*

Thefe are not the only advantages, which the natives of *Arabia* enjoy above the inhabitants of moſt other countries ; they preferve to this day the manners and cuftoms of their anceſtors, who, by their own account, were fettled in the province of *Yemen* above three thoufand years ago: they have never been wholly fubdued by any nation ; and though the admiral of *Selim the Firſt* made a defcent on their coaſt, and exacted a tribute from the people of *Aden,* yet the *Arabians* only keep up a fhow
of

of allegiance to the fultan, and act, on every important occafion, in open defiance of his power, relying on
the fwiftnefs of their horfes, and the vaft extent of their
forefts, in which an invading enemy muft foon perifh:
but here I muft be underftood to fpeak of thofe *Arabians*,
who, like the old *Nomades*, dwell conftantly in their
tents, and remove from place to place according to the
feafons; for the inhabitants of the cities, who traffick
with the merchants of Europe in fpices, perfumes, and
coffee, muft have loft a great deal of their ancient fimplicity: the others have, certainly, retained it; and,
except when their tribes are engaged in war, fpend their
days in watching their flocks and camels, or in repeating
their native fongs, which they pour out almoft extem-
pore, profeffing a contempt for the ftately pillars, and
folemn buildings of the cities, compared with the natural charms of the country, and the coolnefs of their
tents: thus they pafs their lives in the higheft pleafure
of which they have any conception, in the contemplation of the moft delightful objects, and in the enjoyment
of perpetual fpring; for we may apply to part of *Arabia*
that elegant couplet of *Waller* in his poem of the *Summer ifland*,

The gentle fpring, that but falutes us here,
Inhabits there, and courts them all the year.

Yet the heat of the fun, which muft be very intenfe
in a climate fo near the line, is tempered by the fhade

of

of the trees, that overhang the valleys, and by a
number of fresh streams, that flow down the mountains: hence it is, that almost all their notions of *felicity*
are taken from *freshness*, and *verdure*; and it is a maxim
among them that the three most charming objects in
nature are, *a green meadow, a clear rivulet, and a beautiful woman,* and that the view of these objects at the
same time affords the greatest delight imaginable. *Mahomed* was so well acquainted with the maxim of his coun-
trymen, that he described the pleasures of heaven to them,
under the allegory of *cool fountains, green bowers, and
black-eyed girls,* as the word *Houri* literally signifies in
Arabick; and in the chapter of the *Morning*, towards the
end of his *Alcoran*, he mentions a garden, called *Irem*,
which is no less celebrated by the *Asiatick* poets than that
of the *Hesperides* by the *Greeks:* it was planted, as the
commentators say, by a king, named *Shedad*, and was
once seen by an *Arabian*, who wandered very far into
the deserts in search of a lost camel: it was, probably, a
name invented by the impostor, as a type of a future
state of happiness. Now it is certain that the genius
of every nation is not a little affected by their climate;
for, whether it be that the immoderate heat disposes the
Eastern people to a life of indolence, which gives them
full leisure to cultivate their talents, or whether the
sun has a real influence on the imagination, (as one
would suppose that the ancients believed, by their making
Apollo the god of poetry) whatever be the cause, it has

always

always been remarked, that the *Afiaticks* excel the inhabitants of our colder regions in the livelinefs of their
fancy, and the richnefs of their invention.

   To carry this fubjeft one ftep farther: as the *Arabians*
are fuch admirers of *beauty,* and as they enjoy fuch eafe
and leifure, they muft naturally be fufceptible of *that
paffion,* which is the true fpring and fource of agreeable
poetry; and we find, indeed, that *love* has a greater fhare
in their poems than any other paffion : it feems to be always uppermoft in their minds; and there is hardly an
elegy, a panegyrick, or even a fatire, in their language,
which does not begin with the complaints of an unfortu-
nate, or the exultations of a fuccefsful, lover.   It fometimes happens, that the young men of one tribe are in
love with the damfels of another ; and, as the tents are
frequently removed on a fudden, the lovers are often fe-
parated in the progrefs of the courtfhip: hence almoft all
the *Arabick* poems open in this manner; the author be-
wails the fudden departure of his miftrefs, Hinda, Maia,
Zeineb, or Azza, and defcribes her beauty, comparing her
ufually to a wanton fawn, that plays among the aromatick
fhrubs; his friends endeavour to comfort him, but he re-
fufes confolation; he declares his refolution of vifiting
his beloved, though the way to her tribe lie through a
dreadful wildernefs, or even through a den of lions; here
he commonly gives a defcription of the horfe or camel,
upon which he defigns to go, and thence paffes, by an
eafy tranfition, to the principal fubjeft of his poem, whe-
                                                         ther

ther it be the praife of his own tribe, or a fatire on the
timidity of his friends, who refufe to attend him in his
expedition; though very frequently the piece turns wholly
upon love.   But it is not fufficient that a nation have a
genius for poetry, unlefs they have the advantage of a
rich and beautiful language, that their expreffions may be
worthy of their fentiments; the *Arabians* have this advantage alfo in a high degree : their language is expreffive,
ftrong, fonorous, and the moft copious, perhaps, in the
world; for, as almoft every tribe had many words ap-
propriated to itfelf, the poets, for the convenience of
their meafure, or fometimes for their fingular beauty,
made ufe of them all, and, as the poems became popular,
thefe words were by degrees incorporated with the whole
language, like a number of little ftreams, which meet together in one channel, and, forming a moft plentiful
river, flow rapidly into the fea.

If this way of arguing *à priori* be admitted in the prefent cafe, (and no fingle man has a right to infer the merit
of the *Eaftern* poetry from the poems themfelves, becaufe
no fingle man has a privilege of judging for all the reft),
if the foregoing argument have any weight, we muft con-
clude that the *Arabians*, being perpetually converfant
with the moft beautiful objects, fpending a calm and
agreeable life in a fine climate, being extremely addicted
to the fofter paffions, and having the advantage of a language fingularly adapted to poetry, muft be naturally excellent poets, provided that their *manners* and *cuftoms* be
                                                    favourable

favourable to the cultivation of that art; and that they are highly fo, it will not be difficult to prove.

The fondnefs of the *Arabians* for poetry, and the refpect which they fhow to poets, would be fcarce believed, if we were not affured of it by writers of great authority: the principal occafions of rejoicing among them were formerly, and, very probably, are to this day, the birth of a boy, the foaling of a mare, the arrival of a gueft, and the rife of a poet in their tribe : when a young *Arabian* has compofed a good poem, all the neighbours pay their compliments to his family, and congratulate them upon having a relation capable of recording their actions, and of recommending their virtues to pofterity. At the beginning of the feventh century, the *Arabick* language was brought to a high degree of perfection by a fort of poetical academy, that ufed to affemble at ftated times, in a place called *Ocadh*, where every poet produced his beft compofition, and was fure to meet with the applaufe that it deferved : the moft excellent of thefe poems were tranfcribed in characters of gold upon *Egyptian* paper, and hung up in the temple of Mecca, whence they were named *Modhahebat*, or *Golden*, and *Moallakat*, or *Sufpended :* the poems of this fort were called *Caffeida's* or *eclogues,* * feven of which are preferved in our libraries, and are confidered as the fineft that were written before the time

* I have a fine copy of thefe feven poems, clearly tranfcribed with explanatory notes: the names of the feven poets are, *Amralkeis, Tarafa, Zoheir, Lebid, Antara, Amru,* and *Hareth.*

of

of *Mahomed*: the fourth of them, compofed by *Lebid*, is purely paftoral, and extremely like the *Alexis* of *Virgil*, but far more beautiful, becaufe it is more agreeable to nature: the poet begins with praifing the charms of the fair *Novâra*, (a word which in *Arabick* fignifies *a timorous fawn*,) but inveighs againft her unkindnefs; he then interweaves a defcription of his young camel, which he compares for its fwiftnefs to a ftag, purfued by the hounds; and takes occafion afterwards to mention his own riches, accomplifhments, liberality, and valour, his noble birth, and the glory of his tribe: the diction of this poem is eafy and fimple, yet elegant, the numbers flowing and mufical, and the fentiments wonderfully natural; as the learned reader will fee by the following paffage, which I fhall attempt to imitate in verfe, that the merit of the poet may not be wholly loft in a verbal tranflation:

Bel enti la tadrina cam mi'lleilatin,

Thalkin ledhidhin lahwoha wa nedamoha,

Kad bitto fameroha, wa ghayati tajerin

Wafaito idh rofiat, wa azza medamoha,

Befabuhi fafiatin wajadhbi carinatin,

Be mowatterin, taâta leho maan ibhamoha,

Bacarto hajataha' ddajaji befohratin,

Leoalla minha heina bahba neyamoha.

But

But ah! thou know'st not in what youthful play
Our nights, beguil'd with pleasure, swam away;
Gay songs, and cheerful tales, deceiv'd the time,
And circling goblets made a tuneful chime;
Sweet was the draught, and sweet the blooming maid,
Who touch'd her lyre beneath the fragrant shade;
We sip'd till morning purpled every plain;
The damsels slumber'd, but we sip'd again:
The waking birds, that sung on every tree
Their early notes, were not so blithe as we.

The *Mahomedan* writers tell a story of this poet, which deserves to be mentioned here: it was a custom, it seems among the old *Arabians,* for the most eminent versifiers to hang up some chosen couplets on the gate of the temple, as a publick challenge to their brethren, who strove to answer them before the next meeting at *Ocadh,* at which time the whole assembly used to determine the merit of them all, and gave some mark of distinction to the author of the finest verses. Now *Lebid,* who, we are told, had been a violent opposer of *Mahomed,* fixed a poem on the gate, beginning with the following distich, in which he apparently meaned to reflect upon the new religion:

Ila cullo sheion ma khala Allah bathilon,
Wa cullo naimon la mahaloho zailon.

That

That is; *Are not all things vain, which come not from God?* *and will not all honours decay, but those, which He confers?* These lines appeared so sublime, that none of the poets ventured to answer them; till *Mahomed,* who was himself a poet, having composed a new chapter of his *Alcoran,* (the second, I think,) placed the opening of it by the side of *Lebid's* poem, who no sooner read it, than he declared it to be something divine, confessed his own inferiority, tore his verses from the gate, and embraced the religion of his rival; to whom he was afterwards extremely useful in replying to the satires of *Amralkeis,* who was continually attacking the doctrine of *Mahomed:* the *Asiaticks* add, that their lawgiver acknowledged some time after, that no heathen poet had ever produced a nobler distich than that of *Lebid* just quoted.

There are a few other collections of ancient *Arabick* poetry; but the most famous of them is called *Hamassa,* and contains a number of *epigrams, odes,* and *elegies,* composed on various occasions: it was compiled by *Abu Temam,* who was an excellent poet himself, and used to say, that *fine sentiments delivered in prose were like gems scattered at random, but that, when they were confined in a poetical measure, they resembled bracelets, and strings of pearls.* When the religion and language of *Mahomed* were spread over the greater part of *Asia,* and the maritime countries of *Africa,* it became a fashion for the poets of *Persia, Syria, Egypt, Mauritania,* and even of *Tartary,* to write in *Arabick*; and the most beautiful verses in that idiom,

composed

composed by the brighteft genius's of thofe nations, are to be feen in a large mifcellany, entitled *Yateima*; though many of their works are tranfcribed feparately : it will be needlefs to fay much on the poetry of the *Syrians*, *Tartarians*, and *Africans*, fince moft of the arguments, before ufed in favour of the *Arabs*, have equal weight with refpect to the other *Mahomedans*, who have done little more than imitate their ftyle, and adopt their expreffions; for which reafon alfo I fhall dwell the fhorter time on the gènius and manners of the *Perfians*, *Turks*, and *Indians*.

The great empire, which we call *Perfia*, is known to its natives by the name of *Iran*; fince the word *Perfia* belongs only to a particular province, the ancient *Perfis*, and is very improperly applied by us to the whole kingdom : but, in compliance with the cuftom of our geographers, I fhall give the name of *Perfia* to that celebrated country, which lies on one fide between the *Cafpian* and *Indian* feas, and extends on the other from the mountains of *Candahar*, or *Paropamifus*, to the confluence of the rivers *Cyrus* and *Araxes*, containing about twenty degrees from fouth to north, and rather more from eaft to weft.

In fo vaft a tract of land there muft needs be a great variety of climates : the fouthern provinces are no lefs unhealthy and fultry, than thofe of the north are rude and unpleafant ; but in the interiour parts of the empire the air is mild and temperate, and from the beginning of

N May

May to September, there is fcarce a cloud to be feen in
the fky : the remarkable calmnefs of the fummer nights,
and the wonderful fplendour of the moon and ftars in that
country, often tempt the *Perfians* to fleep on the tops of
their houfes, which are generally flat, where they cannot
but obferve the figures of the conftellations, and the various appearances of the heavens; and this may in fome
meafure account for the perpetual allufions of their poets,
and rhetoricians, to the beauty of the heavenly bodies.
We are apt to cenfure the oriental ftyle for being fo full
of metaphors taken from the fun and moon : this is afcribed by fome to the bad tafte of the *Afiaticks*; *the works of
the Perfians,* fays M. *de Voltaire, are like the titles of their
kings, in which the fun and moon are often introduced :* but
they do not reflect that every nation has a fet of images,
and expreffions, peculiar to itfelf, which arife from the
difference of its climate, manners, and hiftory. There
feems to be another reafon for the frequent allufions of the
Perfians to the fun, which may, perhaps, be traced from
the old language and popular religion of their country :
thus *Mihridâd,* or *Mithridates,* fignifies *the gift of the fun,*
and anfwers to the *Theodorus* and *Diodati* of other nations.
As to the titles of the *Eaftern* monarchs, which feem, indeed, very extravagant to our ears, they are merely for-
mal, and no lefs void of meaning than thofe of *European*
princes, in which *ferenity* and *highnefs* are often attributed
to the moft *gloomy,* and *low-minded* of men.

The

The midland provinces of *Perſia* abound in fruits and flowers of almoſt every kind, and, with proper culture, might be made the garden of *Aſia:* they are not watered, indeed, by any conſiderable river, ſince the *Tigris* and *Euphrates*, the *Cyrus* and *Araxes*, the *Oxus*, and the five branches of the *Indus*, are at the fartheſt limits of the kingdom; but the natives, who have a turn for agriculture, ſupply that defect by artificial canals, which ſufficiently temper the dryneſs of the ſoil: but in ſaying they *ſupply* that defect, I am falling into a common errour, and repreſenting the country, not as it *is* at preſent, but as it *was* a century ago; for a long ſeries of civil wars and maſſacres have now deſtroyed the chief beauties of *Perſia*, by ſtripping it of its moſt induſtrious inhabitants.

The ſame difference of climate, that affects the air and ſoil of this extenſive country, gives a variety alſo to the perſons and temper of its natives: in ſome provinces they have dark complexions, and harſh features; in others they are exquiſitely fair, and well-made; in ſome others, nervous and robuſt: but the general character of the nation is that *ſoftneſs*, and *love of pleaſure*, that *indolence* and *effeminacy*, which have made them an eaſy prey to all the weſtern and northern ſwarms, that have from time to time invaded them. Yet they are not wholly void of martial ſpirit; and, if they are not naturally brave, they are at leaſt extremely docile, and might, with proper diſcipline, be made excellent ſoldiers: but the greater

part

part of them, in the fhort intervals of peace that they
happen to enjoy, conftantly fink into a ftate of inactivity,
and pafs their lives in a pleafurable, yet ftudious, retire-
ment; and this may be one reafon, why *Perfia* has produced more writers of every kind, and chiefly *poets*, than
all *Europe* together, fince their way of life gives them
leifure to purfue thofe arts, which cannot be cultivated
to advantage, without the greateft calmnefs and ferenity
of mind: and this, by the way, is one caufe, among
many others, why the poems in the preceding collection
are lefs finifhed; fince they were compofed, not in bowers
and fhades, by the fide of rivulets or fountains, but
either amidft the confufion of a metropolis, the hurry of
travel, the diffipation of publick places, the avocations
of more neceffary ftudies, or the attention to more ufeful parts of literature. To return: there is a manufcript
at *Oxford* * containing *the lives of an hundred and thirty
five of the fineft Perfian poets,* moft of whom left very
ample collections of their poems behind them: but the
verfifiers, and *moderate poets,* if *Horace* will allow any
fuch men to exift, are without number in *Perfia.*

This delicacy of their lives and fentiments has infenfi-
bly affected their language, and rendered it the fofteft, as
it is one of the richeft, in the world: it is not poffible to
convince the reader of this truth, by quoting a paffage
from a *Perfian* poet in *European* characters; fince the

---

* In Hyperoo Bodl. 128. There is a prefatory difcourfe to this
curious work, which comprifes the lives of ten *Arabian* poets.

fweetnefs

ſweetneſs of ſound cannot be determined by the ſight, and many words, which are ſoft and muſical in the mouth of a *Perſian*, may appear very harſh to our eyes, with a number of conſonants and gutturals : it may not, however, be abſurd to ſet down in this place, an Ode of the poet *Hafez*, which, if it be not ſufficient to prove the delicacy of his language, will at leaſt ſhow the livelineſs of his poetry :

Ai bad neſîmi yâr dari,
Zan nefheï muſhcôâr dari :
Zinhar mecun diraz-deſti !
Ba turreï o che câr dari ?
Ai gul, to cujâ wa ruyi zeibaſh ?
O taza, wa to kharbâr dari.
Nerkes, to cujâ wa cheſhmi meſteſh ?
O ſerkhoſh, wa to khumâr dari.
Ai ſeru, to ba kaddi bulendeſh,
Der bagh che iytebâr dari ?
Ai akl, to ba wujûdi iſhkeſh
Der deſt che ikhtiyâr dari ?
Rihan, to cujâ wa khatti ſebzeſh ?
O muſhc, wa to ghubâr dari.
Ruzi bureſi bewaſli Hafez,
Gher takati yntizâr dari.

N 3   That

That is, word for word: *O sweet gale, thou bearest the fragrant scent of my beloved; thence it is that thou hast this musky odour. Beware! do not steal: what hast thou to do with her tresses? O rose, what art thou, to be compared with her bright face? She is fresh, and thou art rough with thorns. O narcissus, what art thou in comparison of her languishing eye? Her eye is only sleepy, but thou art sick and faint. O pine, compared with her graceful stature, what honour hast thou in the garden? O wisdom, what wouldst thou choose, if to choose were in thy power, in preference to her love? O sweet basil, what art thou, to be compared with her fresh cheeks? they are perfect musk, but thou art soon withered. O Hafez, thou wilt one day attain the object of thy desire, if thou canst but support thy pain with patience.* This little song is not unlike a sonnet, ascribed to *Shake-spear*, which deserves to be cited here, as a proof that the *Eastern* imagery is not so different from the *European* as we are apt to imagine.

The forward violet thus did I chide:

" Sweet thief! whence didst thou steal thy sweet that smells,

" If not from my love's breath? The purple pride,

" Which on thy soft cheek for complexion dwells,

" In my love's veins thou hast too grossly dyed."

The lily I condemned for thy hand,

And buds of marjoram had stol'n thy hair;

The roses fearfully on thorns did stand,

One blushing shame, another white despair;

A

A third, nor red, nor white, had ftol'n of beth,
And to his robb'ry had annex'd thy breath;
But for his theft, in pride of all his growth,
A vengeful canker eat him up to death.
More flow'rs I noted, yet I none could fee,
But fweet or colour it had ftol'n from thee.

The *Perfian* ftyle is faid to be ridiculoufly bombaft, and this fault is imputed to the flavifh fpirit of the nation, which is ever apt to magnify the objects that are placed above it: there are bad writers, to be fure, in every country, and as many in *Afia* as elfewhere; but, if we take the pains to learn the *Perfian* language, we fhall find that thofe authors, who are generally efteemed in *Perfia*, are neither flavifh in their fentiments, nor ridiculous in their expreffions: of which the following paffage in a moral work of *Sadi*, entitled *Boftân*, or, *The Garden*, will be a fufficient proof.

Shinidem ke, der wakti nezi rewan,
Be Hormuz chunin gufti Nufhirewan:
Ki khatir nigehdari derwifhi bafh,
Ne der bendi âfaïfhi khifhi bafh:
Neâfaïd ender diyari to kes,
Chu âfaïfhi khifhi khahi wa bes.

N 4

Neyayid

Ncyayid benezdiki dana pefend,

Shubani khufte, wa gurki der kufpend,

Beru ; pafi derwifhi muhtáji dar,

Ki fhah ez ra'yeti búd táji dar.

Raiyet chu bikheft wa foltan dirakht,

Dirakht, ai pifer, bafhed ez bikhi fakht.

That is ; *I have heard that king Nufhirvan, juft before his death, fpoke thus to his fon Hormuz : Be a guardian, my fon, to the poor and helplefs ; and be not confined in the chains of thy own indolence. No one can be at eafe in thy dominion, while thou feekeft only thy private reft, and fay'ft, It is enough. A wife man will not approve the fhepherd, who fleeps while the wolf is in the fold. Go, my fon, protect thy weak and indigent people ; fince through them is a king raifed to the diadem. The people are the root, and the king is the tree, that grows from it ; and the tree, O my fon, derives its ftrength from the root.*

Are thefe mean fentiments, delivered in pompous language ? Are they not rather worthy of our moft fpirited writers ? And do they not convey a fine leffon for a young king ? Yet *Sadi's* poems are highly efteemed at *Conftantinople*, and at *Ifpahan* ; though, a century or two ago, they would have been fuppreffed in *Europe*, for fpreading, with two ftrong a glare, the light of liberty and reafon,

As

As to the great Epick poem of *Ferdusi*, which was compofed in the tenth century, it would require a very long treatife to explain all its beauties with a minute exactnefs. The whole collection of that poet's works is called *Shabnâma*, and contains the hiftory of *Perfia*, from the earlieft times to the invafion of the *Arabs*, in a feries of very noble poems; the longeft and moft regular of which is an heroic poem of one great and interefting action, namely, *the delivery of Perfia by Cyrus*, from the oppreffions of *Afrafiab*, king of the *Tranfoxan Ta tary*, who, being affifted by the emperours of *India* and *China*, together with all the dæmons, giants, and enchanters of *Afia*, had carried his conquefts very far, and become exceedingly formidable to the *Perfians*. This poem is longer than the *Iliad*; the characters in it are various and ftriking; the figures bold and animated; and the diction every where fonorous, yet noble; polifhed, yet full of fire. A great profufion of learning has been thrown away by fome criticks, in comparing *Homer* with the heroick poets, who have fucceeded him; but it requires very little judgment to fee, that no fucceeding poet whatever can with any propriety be compared with *Homer*: that great father of the *Grecian* poetry and literature, had a genius too fruitful and comprehenfive to let any of the ftriking parts of nature efcape his obfervation; and the poets, who have followed him, have done little more than tranfcribe his images, and give a new drefs to his thoughts. Whatever elegance and refine-

refinements, therefore, may have been introduced into
the works of the moderns, the fpirit and invention of
Homer have ever continued without a rival : for which
reafon I am far from pretending to affert that the poet of
Perfia is equal to that of *Greece*; but there is certainly a
very great refemblance between the works of thofe ex-
traordinary men : both drew their images from nature
herfelf, without catching them only by refle&ion, and
painting, in the manner of the modern poets, *the likenefs
of a likenefs*; and both poffeffed, in an eminent degree,
*that rich and creative invention, which is the very foul of
poetry.*

   As the *Perfians* borrowed their poetical meafures, and
the forms of their poems from the *Arabians*; fo the *Turks*,
when they had carried their arms into *Mefopotamia*, and
Affyria, took their numbers, and their tafte for poetry
from the *Perfians*.

   Græcia capta ferum vi&orem cepit, et artes
   Intulit agrefti *Latio*.

In the fame manner as the *Greek* compofitions were the
models of all the *Roman* writers, fo were thofe of *Perfia*
imitated by the *Turks*, who confiderably polifhed and
enriched their language, naturally barren, by the number
of fimple and compound words, which they adopted from
the *Perfian* and *Arabick*. Lady *Wortley Montagu* very

                                             juftly

juſtly obſerves that *we want thoſe compound words, which are very frequent, and ſtrong in* the *Turkiſh language*; but her interpreters led her into a miſtake in explaining one of them, which ſhe tranſlates *ſtag-eyed*, and thinks a *very lively image of the fire and indifference in the eyes of the royal bride :* now it never entered into the mind of an *Aſiatick* to compare his miſtreſs's eyes to thoſe of a *ſtag*, or to give an image of their *fire and indifference*; the *Turks* mean to expreſs that *fullneſs*, and, at the ſame time, that *ſoft and languiſhing luſtre*, which is peculiar to the eyes of their beautiful women, and which by no means reſembles the unpleaſing wildneſs in thoſe of a ſtag. The original epithet, I ſuppoſe, was * *Abû cheſhm*, or, *with the eyes of a young fawn:* now I take the *Abû* to be the ſame animal with the *Gazâl* of the *Arabians*, and the *Zabi* of the *Hebrews*, to which their poets allude in almoſt every page. I have ſeen one of theſe animals; it is a kind of antelope, exquiſitely beautiful, with eyes uncommonly black and large. This is the ſame ſort of roe, to which *Solomon* alludes in this delicate ſimile : *Thy two breaſts are like two young roes, that are twins, which play among the lilies.*

A very polite ſcholar, who has lately tranſlated ſixteen Odes of *Hafez*, with learned illuſtrations, blames the *Turkiſh* poets for copying the *Perſians* too ſervilely : but, ſurely, they are not more blamable than *Horace*, who not only imitated the meaſures and expreſſions of the

Greeks,

Greeks, but even tranflated, almoft word for word, the brighteft paffages of *Alcæus*, *Anacreon*, and others; he took lefs from *Pindar* than from the reft, becaufe the wildnefs of his numbers, and the obfcurity of his allu-fions, were by no means fuitable to the genius of the *Latin* language: and this may, perhaps, explain his ode to *Julius Antonius*, who might have advifed him to ufe more of *Pindar's* manner in celebrating the victories of *Auguftus.* Whatever we may think of this objection, it is certain that the *Turkish* empire has produced a great number of poets; fome of whom had no fmall merit in their way: the ingenious author juft mentioned affured me, that the *Turkish* fatires of *Ruhi Bagdadi* were very forcible and ftriking, and he mentioned the opening of one of them, which feemed not unlike the manner of *Juvenal.* At the beginning of the laft century, a work was publifhed at *Conftantinople*, containing the fineft verfes of *five hundred and forty-nine Turkish poets*, which proves at leaft that they are fingularly fond of this art, whatever may be our opinion of their fuccefs in it.

The defcendants of *Tamerlane* carried into *India* the language and poetry of the *Perfians*; and the *Indian* poets to this day compofe their verfes in imitation of them. The beft of their works, that have paffed through my hands, are thofe of *Huzein*, who lived fome years ago at *Benáres*, with a great reputation for his parts and learning, and was known to the *English*, who refided
there,

ESSAY I.

there, by the name of *the Philosopher*. His poems are elegant and lively, and one of them, *on the departure of his friends*, would fuit our language admirably well, but is too long to be inferted in this effay. The *Indians* are foft and voluptuous, but artful and infincere, at leaft to the *Europeans*, whom, to fay the truth, they have had no great reafon of late years to admire for the oppofite virtues: but they are fond of poetry, which they learned from the *Perfians*, and may, perhaps, before the clofe of the century, be as fond of a more formidable art, which they will learn from the *Englifh*.

I muft once more. requeft, that, in beftowing thefe praifes on the writings of *Afia*, I may not be thought to derogate from the merit of the *Greek* and *Latin* poems, which have juftly been admired in every age; yet I cannot but think that our *European* poetry has fubfifted too long on the perpetual repetition of the fame images, and inceffant allufions to the fame fables: and it has been my endeavour for feveral years to inculcate this truth, *That, if the principal writings of the Afiaticks, which are repofited in our publick libraries, were printed with the ufual advantage of notes and illuftrations, and if the languages of the Eaftern nations were ftudied in our places of education, where every other branch of ufeful knowledge is taught to perfection, a new and ample field would be open for fpeculation; we fhould have a more extenfive infight into the hiftory*

of

of the human mind, we should be furnished with a new set of images and similitudes, and a number of excellent compositions would be brought to light, which future scholars might explain, and future poets might imitate.

ESSAY

E S S A Y   II.

On the Arts, commonly called Imitative.

IT is the fate of thofe maxims, which have been thrown out by very eminent writers, to be received implicitly by moft of their followers, and to be repeated a thoufand times, for no other reafon, than becaufe they once dropped from the pen of a fuperiour genius: one of thefe is the affertion of *Ariftotle*, that *all poetry confifts in imitation*, which has been fo frequently echoed from author to author, that it would feem a kind of arrogance to controvert it; for almoft all the philofophers and criticks, who have written upon the fubject of *poetry, mufick,* and *painting,* how little foever they may agree in fome points, feem of one mind in confidering them as arts merely *imitative:* yet it muft be clear to any one, who examines what paffes in his own mind, that he is affected

by

by the fineft *poems, pieces of mufick,* and *pictures,* upon a
principle, which, whatever it be, is entirely diflinct from
imitation.   *M. le Batteux* has attempted to prove that all
the fine arts have a relation to this common principle of
imitating: but, whatever be faid of *painting,* it is probable, that *poetry* and *mufick* had a nobler origin; and, if
the firft language of man was not both *poetical* and
mufical, it is certain, at leaft, that in countries, where
no kind of *imitation* feems to be much admired, there are
poets and *muficians* both by nature and by art: as in fome
Mahometan nations; where *fculpture* and *painting* are for-
bidden by the laws, where *dramatick poetry* of every fort
is wholly unknown, yet, where the pleafing arts, *of
expreffing the paffions in verfe, and of enforcing that expreffion by melody,* are cultivated to a degree of enthufiafm.
It fhall be my endeavour in this paper to prove, that,
though *poetry* and *mufick* have, certainly, a power of *imitating* the manners of men, and feveral objects in nature,
yet, that their greateft effect is not produced by *imitation,*
but by a very different principle; which muft be fought
for in the deepeft receffes of the human mind.

To ftate the queftion properly, we muft have a clear
notion of what we mean by *poetry and mufick;* but we
cannot give a precife definition of them, till we have
made a few previous remarks on their origin, their relation to each other, and their difference.

It

It feems probable then that *poetry* was originally no more than a ftrong, and animated expreffion of the human paffions, of *joy* and *grief*, *love* and *hate*, *admiration* and *anger*, fometimes pure and unmixed, fometimes varioufly modified and combined: for, if we obferve the *voice* and *accents* of a perfon affected by any of the violent paffions, we fhall perceive fomething in them very nearly approaching to *cadence* and *meafure*; which is remarkably the cafe in the language of a vehement *Orator*, whofe talent is chiefly converfant about *praife* or *cenfure*; and we may collect from feveral paffages in *Tully*, that the fine fpeakers of old *Greece* and *Rome* had a fort of rhythm in their fentences, lefs regular, but not lefs melodious, than that of the poets.

If this idea be juft, one would fuppofe that the moft ancient fort of poetry confifted in *praifing the Deity*; for if we conceive a being, created with all his faculties and fenfes, endued with fpeech and reafon, to open his eyes in a moft delightful plain, to view for the firft time the ferenity of the fky, the fplendour of the fun, the verdure of the fields and woods, the glowing colours of the flowers, we can hardly believe it poffible, that he fhould refrain from burfting into an extafy of *joy*, and pouring his praifes to the creator of thofe wonders, and the author of his happinefs. This *kind of poetry* is ufed in all nations; but as it is the fublimeft of all, when it is applied to its true object, fo it has often been perverted to impious purpofes by pagans and idolaters: every one knows that the *dramatick poetry* of the *Europeans* took its

O rife

rife from the fame fpring, and was no more at firft than a fong in praife of *Bacchus*; fo that the only fpecies of poetical compofition, (if we except the Epick) which can in any fenfe be called *imitative*, was deduced from a natural emotion of the mind, in which *imitation* could not be at all concerned.

The next fource of poetry was, probably, *love*, or the mutual inclination, which naturally fubfifts between the fexes, and is founded upon perfonal *beauty:* hence arofe the moft agreeable *odes*, and love-fongs, which we admire in the works of the ancient lyrick poets, not filled, like our *fonnets* and *madrigals*, with the infipid babble of *darts*, and *Cupids*, but fimple, tender, natural; and confifting of fuch unaffected endearments, and mild complaints,

     * Teneri fdegni, e placide e tranquille
      Repulfe, e cari vezzi, e liete paci,

as we may fuppofe to have paffed between the firft lovers in a ftate of innocence, before the refinements of fociety, and the reftraints, which they introduced, had made the paffion of *love* fo fierce, and impetuous, as it is faid to have been in *Dido*, and certainly was in *Sappho*, if we may take her own word for it †.

   * Two lines of *Taffo*.

   † See the ode of *Sappho* quoted by *Longinus*, and tranflated by *Boileau*.

                       The

The *grief*, which the firſt inhabitants of the earth muſt have felt at the death of their deareſt friends, and relations, gave riſe to another ſpecies of poetry, which originally, perhaps, confiſted of ſhort *dirges*, and was afterwards lengthened into *elegies*.

As ſoon as vice began to prevail in the world, it was natural for the wiſe and virtuous to expreſs their *deteſta-tion* of it in the ſtrongeſt manner, and to ſhow their *re-ſentment* againſt the corrupters of mankind : hence *moral poetry* was derived, which, at firſt, we find, was ſevere and paſſionate ; but was gradually melted down into cool precepts of morality, or exhortations to virtue : we may reaſonably conjecture that *Epick poetry* had the ſame ori-gin, and that the examples of heroes and kings were in-troduced, to illuſtrate ſome moral truth, by ſhowing the lovelineſs and advantages of virtue, or the many misfor-tunes that flow from vice.

Where there is vice, which is *deteſtable* in itſelf, there muſt be *hate*, ſince *the ſtrongeſt antipathy in nature*, as *Mr. Pope* aſſerted in his writings, and proved by his whole life, *ſubſiſts between the good and the bad :* now this paſſion was the ſource of that poetry, which we call *Satire*, very improperly, and corruptly, ſince the *Satire* of the *Romans* was no more than a moral piece, which

they

they entitled *Satura* or *Satyra*, * intimating, that the poem, like *a dish of fruit and corn offered to Ceres*, contained a variety and plenty of fancies and figures; whereas the true *invectives* of the ancients were called *Iambi*, of which we have several examples in *Catullus*, and in the *Epodes* of *Horace*, who imitated the very measures and manner of *Archilochus*.

These are the principal sources of *poetry*; and of *music* also, as it shall be my endeavour to show: but it is first neceffary to fay a few words on *the nature of found*; a very copious fubject, which would require a long differtation to be accurately difcuffed. Without entering into a difcourfe on the *vibrations of chords*, or *the undulations of the air*, it will be fufficient for our purpofe to obferve that there is a great difference between *a common found*, and *a mufical found*, which confifts chiefly in this, that the former is fimple and entire in itfelf like a *point*, while the latter is always accompanied with other founds, without ceafing to be *one*; like a *circle*, which is an entire figure, though it is generated by a multitude of points flowing, at equal diftances, round a common centre. Thefe acceffory founds, which are caufed · by the aliquots of a fonorous body vibrating at once, are called *Harmonicks*, and the whole fyftem of modern *Harmony* depends upon them; though it were eafy to prove that the fyftem is unnatural, and only made tolerable to the ear by habit: for whenever we ftrike the perfect

* Some Latin words were fpelled either with an *u* or a *y*, as *Sulla* or *Sylla*.

accord

accord on a harpfichord or an organ, the harmonicks of the third and fifth have alfo their own harmonicks, which are diffonant from the principal note : Thefe horrid' diffonances are, indeed, almoft overpowered by the *natural harmonicks* of the principal chord, but that does not -prove them agreeable. Since nature has given us a delightful harmony of her own, why fhould we deftroy it by the additions of art ? It is like thinking   .

———— to paint the lily, .

And add a perfume to the violet.   .

Now let us conceive that fome vehement paffion is expreffed in ftrong words, exactly meafured, and pronounced, *in a common voice*, in juft cadence, and with proper accents, fuch an expreffion of the paffion will be *genuine poetry*; and the famous ode.of *Sappho* is allowed to be fo in the ftricteft fenfe : but if the fame ode, with all its natural accents, were expreffed in a *mufical voice*, (that is, in founds accompanied with their *Harmonicks*) if it were fung in due time and meafure, in a fimple and pleafing tune, that added force to the words without ftifling them, it would then be *pure and original mufick*; not merely foothing to the ear, but affecting to the heart ; not an *imitation* of nature, but the voice of nature herfelf. But there is another point in which *mufick* muft refemble *poetry*, or it will lofe a confiderable part of its effect: we all muft have obferved, that a fpeaker, agitated with

O 3   paffion,

paffion, or an actor, who is, indeed, ftrictly an *imitator*, are perpetually changing the tone and pitch of their voice, as the fenfe of their words varies : it may be worth while to examine how this variation is exprefied in *mufick*. Every body knows that the mufical fcale confifts of feven notes, above which we find a fucceffion of fimilar founds repeated in the fame order, and above that, other fucceffions, as far as they can be continued by the human voice, or diftinguifhed by the human ear : now each of thefe feven founds has no more meaning, when it is heard feparately, than a fingle letter of the alphabet would have ; and it is only by their fucceffion, and their relation to one principal found, that they take any rank in the fcale ; or differ from each other, except as they are *graver*, or more *acute :* but in the regular fcale each interval affumes a proper character, and every note ftands related to the firft or principal one by various proportions. Now *a feries of founds relating to one leading note* is called a *mode*, or a *tone*, and, as there are twelve femitones in the fcale, each of which may be made in its turn the leader of a mode, it follows that there are twelve modes ; and each of them has a peculiar character, arifing from the pofition of the *modal* note, and from fome minute difference in the ratio's, as of 81 to 80, or a comma ; for there are fome intervals, which cannot eafily be rendered on our inftruments, yet have a furprizing effect in *modulation*, or in the tranfitions from one mode to another.

The

The *modes* of the ancients are faid to have had a wonderful effect over the mind ; and *Plato*, who permits the
Dorian in his imaginary republick, on account of its
calmnefs and gravity, excludes the *Lydian*, becaufe of
its languid, tender, and effeminate character: not that
any feries of mere founds has a power of raifing or foothing the paffions, but each of thefe modes was appropri-
ated to a particular kind of poetry, and a particular inftrument; and the chief of them, as the *Dorian, Phrygian,
Lydian, Ionian, Eolian, Locrian,* belonging originally to
the nations, from which they took their names : thus
the *Phrygian mode*, which was ardent and impetuous, was
ufually accompanied with trumpets, and the *Mixolydian,*
which, if we believe *Ariftoxenus*, was invented by *Sappho,*
was probably confined to the pathetick and tragick ftyle :
that thefe modes had a relation to *poetry*, as well as to
mufick, appears from a fragment of *Lafus*, in which he
fays, *I fing of Ceres, and her daughter Melibœa, the confort of Pluto, in the Eolian mode, full of gravity*; and
Pindar calls one of his *Odes* an *Eolian fong.*   If the
Greeks furpaffed us in the ftrength of their modulations,
we have an advantage over them in our *minor fcale*, which
fupplies us with twelve new modes, where the two femitones are removed from their natural pofition between the
third and fourth, the feventh and eighth notes, and
placed between the fecond and third, the fifth and fixth ;
this change of the femitones, by giving a minor third to
the *modal* note, foftens the general expreffion of the

mode,

mode, and adapts it admirably to fubjects of *grief* and *affliction:* the minor mode of D is tender, that of C, with three flats, plaintive, and that of F, with four, pathetick and mournful to the higheft degree, for which reafon it was chofen by the excellent *Pergolefi* in his *Stabat Mater.* Now thefe twenty-four modes, artfully interwoven, and changed as often as the fentiment changes, may, it is evident, exprefs all the variations in the voice of a fpeaker, and give an additional beauty to the accents of a poet. Confiftently with the foregoing principles, .we may define *original and native poetry* to be *the language of the violent paffions, expreffed in exact mea-fure, with ftrong accents and fignificant words;* and *true mufick* to be no more than *poetry, delivered in a fucceffion of harmonious founds, fo difpofed as to pleafe the ear.* It is in this view only that we muft confider the mufick of the ancient *Greeks,* or attempt to account for its amazing effects, which we find related by the graveft hiftorians, and philofophers; it was wholly .paffionate or defcriptive, and fo clofely united to poetry, that it never obftructed, but always increafed its influence; whereas our boafted harmony, with all its fine accords, and numerous parts, paints nothing, expreffes nothing, fays nothing to the heart, and confequently can only give more or lefs plea-fure, to one of our fenfes; and no reafonable man will ferioufly prefer a tranfitory pleafure, which muft foon end in fatiety, or even in difguft, to a delight of the foul, arifing from fympathy, and founded on the na-tural paffions, always lively, always interefting, always

tranfport-

tranfporting. The old divifions of mufick into *celeftial* and *earthly, divine* and *human, active* and *contemplative, intellective* and *oratorial,* were founded rather upon meta- phors, and chimerical analogies, than upon any real diftinctions in nature; but the want of making a diftinc- tion between *mufick of mere founds,* and the *mufick of the paffions,* has been the perpetual fource of confufion and contradictions both among the ancients and the moderns: nothing can be more oppofite in many points than the fyftems of *Rameau* and *Tartini,* one of whom afferts that melody fprings from harmony, and the other deduces harmony from melody; and both are in the right, if the firft fpeaks only of that mufick, which took its rife from *the multiplicity of founds heard at once in the fonorous body,* and the fecond, of that, which rofe from *the ac- cents and inflexions of the human voice, animated by the paffions:* to decide, as *Rouffau* fays, whether of thefe two fchools ought to have the preference, we need only afk a plain queftion, Was the voice made for the inftru- ments, or the inftruments for the voice?

. In defining what true poetry *ought to be,* according to our principles, we have defcribed what it really *was* among the *Hebrews,* the *Greeks* and *Romans,* the *Arabs* and *Perfians.* The lamentation of *David,* and his fa- cred odes, or pfalms, the fong of *Solomon,* the prophecies of *Ifaiah, Jeremiah,* and the other infpired writers, are truly and ftrictly poetical; but what did *David* or *Solo- mon* imitate in their divine poems? A man, who is *really* joyful

joyful or afflicted, cannot be said to *imitate* joy or affliction. The lyrick verses of *Alcæus, Alcman,* and *Ibycus,*
the hymns of *Callimachus,* the elegy of *Moschus* on the
death of *Bion,* are all beautiful pieces of poetry; yet
Alcæus was no *imitator* of love, *Callimachus* was no *imitator* of religious awe and admiration, *Moschus* was no
imitator of grief at the loss of an amiable friend. *Aris-
totle* himself wrote a very poetical elegy on the death of
a man, whom he had loved; but it would be difficult to
say what he imitated in it: " *O virtue, who proposest*
" *many labours to the human race, and art still the alluring*
" *object of our life; for thy charms, O beautiful goddess, it*
" *was, always an envied happiness in Greece even to die, and*
" *to suffer the most painful, the most afflicting evils: such are*
" *the immortal fruits, which thou raisest in our minds;*
" *fruits, more precious than gold, more sweet than the love*
" *of parents, and soft repose: for thee Hercules the son of*
" *Jove, and the twins of Leda, sustained many labours, and*
" *by their illustrious actions sought thy favour; for love of*
" *thee, Achilles and Ajax descended to the mansion of Pluto;*
" *and, through a zeal for thy charms, the prince of Atarnea*
" *also was deprived of the sun's light: therefore shall the*
" *muses, daughters of memory, render him immortal for his*
" *glorious deeds, whenever they sing the god of hospitality, and*
" *the honours due to a lasting friendship.*"

In the preceding collection of poems, there are some
Eastern fables, some *odes,* a *panegyrick,* and an *elegy;* yet
it does not appear to me, that there is the least *imitation*

in

in either of them : *Petrarch* was, certainly, too deeply affected with real *grief*, and the *Perſian* poet was too ſincere a lover, to *imitate* the paſſions of others. As to the reſt, a fable in verſe is no more an *imitation* than a fable in proſe ; and if every poetical narrative, which deſcribes the manners, and relates the adventures of men, be called *imitative*, every romance, and even every hiſtory, muſt be called ſo likewiſe ; ſince many poems are only *romances*, or parts of *hiſtory*, told in a regular meaſure.

What has been ſaid of *poetry*, may with equal force be applied to *muſick*, which is *poetry*, dreſſed to advantage ; and even to *painting*, many ſorts of which are poems to the eye, as all poems, merely deſcriptive, are pictures to the ear : and this way of conſidering them, will ſet the refinements of modern artiſts in their true light ; for the *paſſions*, which were given by nature, never ſpoke in an unnatural form, and no man, truely affected with *love* or *grief*, ever expreſſed the one in an *acroſtick*, or the other in a *fugue :* theſe remains, therefore, of the falſe taſte, which prevailed in the dark ages, ſhould be baniſhed from this, which is enlightened with a juſt one.

It is true, that ſome kinds of painting are ſtrictly *imitative*, as that which is ſolely intended to repreſent the human figure and countenance ; but it will be found, that thoſe pictures have always the greateſt effect, which repreſent reprefent fome *paffion*, as the martyrdom of *St. Agnes* by *Domenichino*, and the various reprefentations of the *Crucifixion* by the fneft mafters of *Italy*; and there can be no doubt, but that the famous *facrifice of Iphigenia* by *Timanthes* was affecting to the higheft degree; which proves, not that painting cannot be faid to *imitate*, but that its moft powerful influence over the mind arifes, like that of the other arts, from *fympathy*.

It is afferted alfo that *defcriptive* poetry, and *defcriptive* mufick, as they are called, are ftrict *imitations*; but, not to infift that mere *defcription* is the meaneft part of both arts, if indeed it belongs to them at all, it is clear, that words and founds have no kind of refemblance to vifible objects : and what is an imitation, but a refemblance of fome other thing ? Befides, no unprejudiced hearer will fay that he finds the fmalleft traces of imitation in the numerous *fugues, counterfugues,* and *divifions,* which rather difgrace than adorn the modern mufick : even founds themfelves are imperfectly imitated by harmony, and, if we fometimes hear *the murmuring of a brook,* or *the chirping of birds* in a concert, we are generally apprifed before-hand of the paffages, where we may expect them. Some eminent muficians, indeed, have been abfurd enough to think of imitating laughter and other noifes, but, if they had fucceeded, they could not have made amends for their want of tafte in attempting it; for fuch ridiculous imitations muft neceffarily deftroy the fpirit and dignity of the fineft poems, which they ought to

illuftrate

illuftrate by a graceful and natural melody. It feems to me, that, as thofe parts of *poetry*, *mufick*, and *painting*, which relate to the paffions, affect by *fympathy*, fo thofe, which are merely defcriptive, act by a kind of *fubftitution*, that is, by raifing in our minds, affections, or fentiments, analogous to thofe, which arife in us, when the refpective objects in nature are prefented to our fenfes. Let us fuppofe that a poet, a mufician, and a painter, are ftriving to give their friend, or patron, a pleafure fimilar to that, which he feels at the fight of a beautiful profpect. The firft will form an agreeable affemblage of lively images, which he will exprefs in fmooth and elegant verfes of a fprightly meafure; he will defcribe the moft delightful objects, and will add to the graces of his defcription a certain delicacy of fentiment, and a fpirit of cheerfulnefs. The mufician, who undertakes to fet the words of the poet, will felect fome mode, which, on his violin, has the character of mirth and gaiety, as the Eolian, or *E flat*, which he will change as the fentiment is varied: he will exprefs the words in a fimple and agreeable melody, which will not difguife, but embellifh them, without aiming at any fugue, or figured harmony: he will ufe the bafs, to mark the modulation more ftrongly, efpecially in the changes; and he will place the *tenour* generally in unifon with the bafs, to prevent too great a diftance between the parts: in the fymphony he will, above all things, avoid a *double melody*, and will apply his variations only to fome acceffory ideas, which the principal part, that is, the voice, could

not

not eafily exprefs : he will not make a number of ufelefs repetitions, becaufe the *paffions* only repeat the fame ex- preffions, and dwell upon the fame fentiments, while *defcription* can only reprefent a fingle objeɛt by a fingle fentence. The painter will defcribe all vifible objeɛts more exaɛtly than his rivals, but he will fall fhort of the other artifts in a very material circumftance ; name- ly, that his pencil, which may, indeed, exprefs a fimple paffion, cannot paint a thought, or draw the fhades of fentiment : he will, however, finifh his landfcape with grace and elegance ; his colours will be rich, and glow- ing ; his perfpeɛtive ftriking ; and his figures will be difpofed with an agreeable variety, but not with confu- fion : above all, he will diffufe over his whole piece fuch a fpirit of livelinefs and feftivity, that the beholder fhall be feized with a kind of rapturous delight, and, for a moment, miftake art for nature.

Thus will each artift gain his end, not by *imitating* the works of nature, but by affuming her power, and caufing the fame effeɛt upon the imagination, which her charms produce to the fenfes : this muft be the chief objeɛt of a poet, a mufician, and a painter, who know that *great effeɛts are not produced by minute details, but by the general fpirit of the whole piece, and that a gaudy compofition may ftrike the mind for a fhort time, but that the beauties of fimplicity are both more delightful, and more per- manent.*

As

As the *paffions* are differently modified in different men, and as even the various objects in nature affect our minds in various degrees, it is obvious, that there muft be a great diverfity in the pleafure, which we receive from the fine arts, whether that pleafure arifes from *fympathy*, or *fubftitution*; and that it were a wild notion in artifts to think of pleafing every reader, hearer, or beholder; fince every man has a particular fet of objects, and a particular inclination, which direct him in the choice of his pleafures, and induce him to confider the productions, both of nature and of art, as more or lefs elegant, in proportion as they give him a greater or fmaller degree of delight: this does not at all contradict the opinion of many able writers, that *there is one uniform ftandard of tafte*; fince the *paffions*, and, confequently, *fympathy*, are generally the fame in all men, till they are weakened by age, infirmity, or other caufes.

If the arguments, ufed in this effay, have any weight, it will appear, that the fineft parts of poetry, mufick, and painting, are expreffive of the *paffions*, and operate on our minds by *fympathy*; that the inferior parts of them are *defcriptive* of natural *objects*, and affect us chiefly by *fubftitution*; that the expreffions of *love*, *pity*, *defire*, and the *tender* paffions, as well as the *defcriptions* of objects that delight the fenfes, produce in the arts what we call the *beautiful*; but that *hate*, *anger*, *fear*, and the *terrible* paffions, as well as objects, which are *unpleafing* to the fenfes,

fenfes, are productive of the *fublime*, when they are aptly expreffed, or defcribed.

Thefe fubjects might be purfued to infinity; but, if they were amply difcuffed, it would be neceffary to write a feries of differtations, inftead of an effay.

THE   END.

www.ingramcontent.com/pod-product-compliance
Lightning Source LLC
Chambersburg PA
CBHW030116030726
47498CB00007B/2405